FLICKER

SUMMER'S HAREM BOOK 3

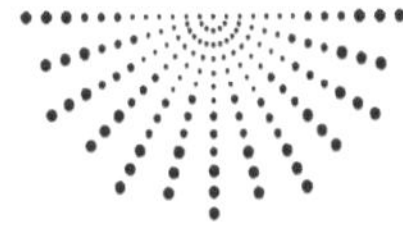

MAGGIE ALABASTER

To Evie. RiP.

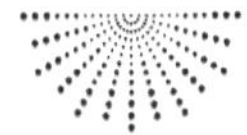

CHAPTER ONE

"**W**ell, fuck," I said.

I wrinkled my nose at the stink of rotted foliage.

Khat's words echoed through my mind.

We're close to the Fae capital. We were gone longer than we thought.

The taint has spread.

The taint has spread.

The taint has...

I felt ill.

"We have to find the last key." Huon's firm voice broke through my thoughts. "Let's get back to the capital. We could all use a bath and a good meal. We'll work out a plan from there."

His face hard as stone, he helped me to my feet. "You look pale."

"It's all that spinning through portals," I replied. "It makes me dizzy." I looked away, but he caught my chin and forced my face back toward him.

"I know you better than that." He locked his gaze on mine. "I know this looks bad, but we will fix this."

I thought he was going to add, "I promise," but he didn't. That was just as well; I would have called him out on it. I knew he wanted to save the Fae realm as much as I did, as much as we *all* did, but this was far worse than we expected.

It might already have been too late.

I pushed that line of thought out of my head. I had to believe we still had time. Anything else would be giving up and I wasn't ready for that. Not yet.

Huon pressed his lips to mine and gave me a slow, lingering kiss.

I was the one who pulled back first.

"We should get home," I told him. I could have stayed locked in that kiss for days, but we had more important matters to deal with. There would be time for all of that later, gods willing.

He nodded and stepped away to pick up his bag from the ground.

"We have to go back." Fletcher's eyes were wide.

The scars on the side of his face stood out against his white skin. "My brother and Jude—"

"I don't know if we can." I still had my fingers curled around the orb.

I opened my hand slowly and let it sit on my palm. It looked like nothing more than a golden ball, with symbols etched on the sides. I thought at it, like I had back in the human realm, but got no response.

"We don't have time," Huon said. He shot Fletcher an apologetic look. "We have to fix things here first."

Fletcher's face turned red. For a moment I thought the gentle human might punch Huon in the face. "But the island was—"

"I *know* the island might sink into the ocean," Huon snapped. "We *did* try to look for them and found no sign. For all we know, they already left."

"The boat was still there." Evidently Fletcher wasn't ready to give up the argument yet.

"I'm aware of that," Huon replied, his voice like chips of ice. "We need to find the second key and save this realm. If we don't, the human realm will also die. We can't go back for two people, and a dog, if it means risking the lives of billions. I'm sorry. We're not going back. That's final."

Huon turned away.

Fletcher looked toward me with a frantic

expression.

I hesitated, then closed my hand over the orb. "I'm sorry, but Huon is right. We will go back and find them, just not today." I lowered my arm to my side and let my shoulders sag.

I really did feel bad, even if Rick was an ass. Jude and his huge dog, Tiny, I considered my friends. I didn't abandon friends. I didn't like doing it now.

Fletcher's mouth worked, but no sound came out. Finally, he nodded and bent to pick up his pack. His body was stiff, as though he was held together by anger, but he would gain nothing by arguing anyway. If the orb wouldn't take us back, he couldn't return, even if Huon agreed to it.

I watched Fletcher for a moment and sighed.

"It is difficult to make the tough calls," Tavar said softly.

I hadn't realised she'd walked up behind me. I jumped and whirled around.

She regarded me with faint amusement. "You and the king made the right call."

"It might be the only call," I told her. "The orb may not work the other way anyway."

She inclined her head slowly. "That is possible. You were right not to try, in case it did. You might end up somewhere unexpected, or unwelcomed."

"Yes, I suppose we might." I didn't tell her I'd tried. Since the orb hadn't responded, the point was moot. Although, I should be careful what I thought about, just in case it changed its mind.

I tucked the golden sphere into my pocket with more haste than might strictly be necessary. Part of me was glad it hadn't worked again. I'd spun through enough portals over the last few days, I didn't want to accidentally suck myself through another.

Tavar looked amused.

I ignored her and moved to stand beside Kale. "Did you know the orb would do that?" I asked.

The dark skinned Fae looked down at me with soft eyes and the slightest hint of a smile.

He nodded slowly, once. "I suspected it might have some abilities, but I was uncertain as to what," he said, his voice a deep rumble. "It's logical that the creation of portals was one of them. The ancients clearly wanted us to return here to find the final key once we'd claimed the first two."

"I feel like a puppet," I sighed. "The ancients might have made those strings a long time ago, but they're still pulling them." I never liked being told what to do. Being controlled by long-dead Fae was no less irritating, however necessary it might be.

"It does seem so," he agreed. "We should be

grateful they did all of this for us. Without them, the realm would certainly die."

I looked around at the sad, dying trees. "They could have made it easier by having all the keys here. We would have found them by now."

Kale took my hand and drew me to him. "We are close," he assured me. "We have the first two. They will guide us to the final key." To my surprise, he pressed a gentle kiss to my lips.

I responded by kissing him back.

"Shouldn't we go and find it then?" Khat interrupted by pushing himself between our ankles. "Why waste more time?"

"We do need to eat," I told the mimicat while I gave him a grimace. Every time Kale and I had a moment, he would appear and disrupt it. I hesitated and frowned.

"Also, I don't feel the key telling me anything." I felt around in my pocket for it, while trying not to touch the orb. I pulled it out. It was silver and small and apart from being warm from my body, looked ordinary.

Kale's eyes widened. He drew out his key. "Also nothing." He sounded bewildered.

"Maybe the last key isn't here?" I glanced toward Tavar. "Is that possible?"

She looked as perplexed as I felt.

"Maybe they just know you're tired and hungry," Huon said.

"And maybe someone changed the rules on us," Saff remarked.

Even though that was what I was thinking, I grimaced at him.

He shrugged. "Someone had to say it. Maybe the orb—"

Huon cut him off. "We could stand here and speculate, or we could do that over a plate of food, and in clean clothes."

"All right, all right." I tucked the key away. "Fletcher?"

"I'll fly with Saff," he replied.

I blinked at him, but nodded. He'd always let me fly him. That he didn't want to now stung, but it was his choice. I supposed we could all do with a break from each other. This journey had put us all under pressure and on edge.

I nodded. "Khat, Tavar, do one of you want to fly with me?" I knew better than to ask them to travel together. Khat wouldn't be likely to forget that trolls ate mimicats, or had in the past. Personally, I thought he would taste stringy and unpleasant, but I had no plans to find out.

"I will," Khat replied. "You annoy me slightly less than the rest of them."

"Uh, all right then." I scooped him up and shrunk him just enough for him to fit comfortably in my arms. "Thanks, I think."

"Yeah, yeah, don't go getting soft on me," he growled. "Not until it's time to eat. Then be as kind as you like."

"I'll be too busy eating," I told him. The more we talked about food, the hungrier I became. My stomach had settled after our whirl through the portal and I was ready to stuff it silly.

"Whatever. Just don't drop me. I would find that objectionable." His ears flicked back and forth slowly.

"I'll try not to." I spread my wings and took off after Huon. He was a few metres in front of me.

Saff followed with a tight-lipped Fletcher, and Tavar traveled with Kale.

I didn't want to look, but my eyes went to the ground below us. To the east, the trees were all dark, sickly greens and browns. We passed by a lake and a river. Where before, healthy foliage lined the banks, now they were all dead or dying.

I exchanged concerned glances with Huon. We had laughed and played in that river only days ago. I had blown up a rose petal and earned my reputation for being able to destroy things. Kale had flown in and saved my ass that day too.

Now, it looked as though the taint had had years to spread.

"We knew it would spread faster after we got the first key," Huon called out to me.

"Yes, but this—" I shook my head.

"I told you we've been gone longer than we planned," Khat said. "Dark magic, it's done something. I can feel it."

I nodded. I wasn't sure what it was, but I also sensed something malevolent. "We will fix this," I said to myself.

"We had better," Khat replied. "This looks as though the realm will be dead in a matter of weeks."

"No pressure," I replied sarcastically.

"Pressure," he replied firmly. "We're facing the end of the world here."

"Right." The closer we came to the Fae capital, the less of the taint we saw. Maybe a twenty-kilometre radius around the capital looked green and lush. If I concentrated on it hard enough, I could almost pretend the whole realm looked like this still.

"Home," I said finally.

The Fae made their homes in small buildings

built into the branches of the trees. The palace was the most ornate of them, and the biggest, although it too was simple. Built just under the canopy, it blended in with it. With dark timber and wide windows, the houses caught every breeze and sat comfortably in their surroundings.

Walkways encircled the trunks, allowing us to move around between the structures, although we could just as easily fly.

Huon landed on one of these, close to the palace.

We dropped down beside him.

"It's quiet," Saff remarked. "You don't think…"

"I don't know," I replied. I put Khat down at my feet. Oh, gods, if we were too late…

Huon led the way up the walkway to the palace.

"Do you sense anything amiss?" Huon asked Khat over his shoulder.

"I sense something very much wrong," Khat replied. "But there are Fae here."

"Then where—" I stopped as several figures stepped out of the palace and started moving toward us.

"Since when do trolls live here?" I aimed the question at Tavar.

She shook her head. "Not since the dawn of the trolls," she replied uneasily.

"Who approaches?" one of the trolls called out. Like most of his kind, his chest was bare. So was the sword in his hand.

Huon drew himself up. "It's King Huon. You'll do well to stand aside and let us in."

The trolls looked at each other in confusion, but none put away their weapon. The leader murmured to one behind him and they both nodded.

"You should come with us," the leader said. "The queen will want to see you."

Huon relaxed immediately. "Of course, my mother will be relieved to see us." He smiled easily, but a chill slid down my spine.

Again, the trolls exchanged looks. The leader jerked his head toward the doorway.

"Come with us," he ordered. His tone suggested he wouldn't allow arguments. This was becoming more and more strange and unsettling.

Huon's grin faltered. "All right, we were going to anyway. You don't need that blade though. I am king here. My mother will explain everything and clear up this misunderstanding."

He paused, then headed inside.

In spite of my misgivings, I followed.

CHAPTER TWO

"Remain here." The troll led us to the throne room and gestured for us to stand and wait. He ducked back out the door, but four trolls stayed, their eyes on us, hands on weapons.

"I didn't exactly expect to be greeted as a hero—" Huon started.

"I did," Saff said. "We've found two—"

As subtle as I could, I gave him a warning look. I didn't know why, but I had the feeling we shouldn't speak about the keys or the orb in front of the trolls. Whatever the hells was going on, we needed to be careful.

"I'm still king here." Huon's eyes flicked toward the door uncertainly.

I tucked my hand around his arm and leaned into him. "I don't know what's happened, but we'll figure it out, all right?" I said softly. "Khat, can you tell how much time has passed?"

Khat lay on the floor licking his feet. He looked up at me and said, "It's hard to say, but I would guess at least five years have gone by while we were away."

I gaped at him for a moment, then closed my mouth so fast my teeth clicked. Five years? It wasn't long in the life of a Fae, but clearly things had changed during our absence.

I glanced at the trolls. If they listened to anything we'd said, they gave no sign. I knew Tavar well enough to know they would have heard every word. They probably memorised them as well, in case they needed to repeat them.

My gaze slid to Tavar. She gave me a faint nod, which confirmed my suspicions. They were listening. But for whom?

The answer to that came soon enough.

"Praise the gods!" Zinnia swept into the room, gown and cape flared out behind her. She walked to me and gave me an embrace. "Sister dear, I thought you were dead."

She leaned back to regard me and we locked eyes.

Oh yes, in spite of her words, she was not happy to see me at all.

Khat hissed at her and she backed away. For a moment, I thought she might kick him. Instead, she turned and climbed the steps to the throne.

She sat.

"What the fuck?" The words were out before I could stop them.

Before Zinnia could respond, Huon stalked toward her.

"What in the name of the seven hells is going on here?" he demanded. "Where is my mother? What are you doing on *my* throne?"

Zinnia reclined, crossed her legs and examined her fingernails. "Your mother, gods keep her soul, passed away three, no, four years ago now. After King Birch died and you disappeared…the poor woman's heart was so broken she couldn't bear to live anymore. One day she was a vibrant Fae, the next she was a shell of herself. Then she was gone."

"What did you do to her?" Huon growled. He curled his hands in fists.

The trolls pulled their swords and pointed the tips toward Huon.

He spread his hands to either side, palms forward. "Easy."

"I did nothing." Zinnia looked slightly amused, as though she'd pictured this moment over and over in her head over the last couple of years. "The healers were called for. They couldn't help. All she could do was to ask for you. But you were gone." She fixed steely eyes on him.

"And now I'm back," Huon said, his voice tight. "I'll thank you to get off my throne."

Zinnia laughed, a sinister tickling sound with no hint of sincerity.

"You forfeited the throne years ago. Oh," she held up a hand, "we waited for you to return, but when the taint spread, someone had to rule." She shrugged. "The throne is mine now."

"Summer, you're right, your sister really is a bitc —" Saff started to say.

I silence him with a warning look.

Zinnia rolled her eyes. "Are you still persisting with that? Your name is Gardenia. It's a perfectly respectable name for a Fae."

"It's awful." I made a face. My parents could have chosen so many from a long list of names. The gods only knew why they picked that one.

"Nevertheless, it is your name and you *will* use it." Zinnia's gaze slipped from me as though the matter was final. She turned her attention to Tavar. "Troll," she said by way of greeting.

"My name is Tavar, your highness," Tavar replied. The first polite response any of us had given to the situation.

"I don't care." Zinnia gave a shake of her head. "When the taint spread, the trolls came to beg for a home. I gave them one." She drew herself up as though she had done some heroic deed. "You serve the Fae now. They are obedient. I expect nothing less from you as well."

Tavar inclined her head. "Yes, your highness," she replied. What she really thought of any of that, I couldn't tell. Her face was her usual tight mask.

Beside her, Saff spluttered. He looked as though he thought she was a traitor.

Zinnia ignored him and for once he didn't say anything more. Instead, she looked toward Fletcher.

"Human. Why are you here?" she demanded.

Fletcher swallowed audibly. "I was dragged here by a magic portal," he replied simply. He was still pale, his mind clearly on his brother, not what might happen to him.

"He's with me," I said firmly. Whatever kind of slavery the trolls were under, I wouldn't have the same happen to Fletcher.

Zinnia smirked. "Of *course* he is," she replied. She

rolled her eyes. "That would be Gardenia, always with the strays." She eyed Khat, who returned the look with equal hostility.

"He's also with me," I said.

"I am with myself," Khat replied, "but the stink of trolls and so many Fae is unbearable. I'll see myself out." He slinked toward the open door and disappeared.

"And you," Zinnia rose and stepped lightly toward Kale. "Who are you with?" She placed the tip of one finger on his burly chest.

He raised his eyebrows at her.

"I am in the company of these fine folk," he replied. Even under these circumstances, his deep rumbly voice made my pulse quicken.

Zinnia narrowed her eyes. "That wasn't what I asked," she said smoothly. "I need a Fae to help make heirs for the kingdom."

"Are you insane?" Huon burst out. "The taint is spreading. The whole realm is going to die, and you're worried about keeping slaves and screwing?"

Zinnia turned to him, her teeth bared. "This from the prince who spent his time drinking, fucking and sleeping, and then *abandoned* the realm!"

Huon flinched. "I didn't abandon it," he said from behind clenched teeth.

"Then where were you?" she asked.

Huon looked at me.

I shook my head.

"We were stuck in the human realm," I said. "We've been trying to get back for years." Better she didn't know we'd been gone for days. Everything was messed up enough without us telling her the details.

Her brow creased. "But you found a way," she said slowly. "Is the human realm also dying?"

I blinked. I fully understood why she would ask, but I didn't know how to respond.

I licked my lips. "It's… at risk as well, yes."

"But not as much as here?" she asked eagerly.

I glanced at Huon. His eyes were wide. Clearly he had no idea how to answer either.

I exhaled through my nose. "It's complicated. Maybe we can talk about it after we rest."

I thought she might refuse, but she nodded. "Troll, you go with the others. The rest of you will have to stay in Gardenia's old room. Everywhere else is full."

"The rest of the Fae are here?" Kale asked.

I could have slapped myself. I had forgotten he wasn't from the capital. Of *course* he had family and friends back at his home village. If the taint had grown, they might have come here as refugees.

"Those who came haven't been turned away," she replied. Again she looked as though she had done something heroic.

Kale nodded. "I will have to seek my family out later."

I put a hand on his arm. "Why don't you go now? I have to talk to my sister anyway. It will probably take a while." And get ugly. Well, uglier than it already was, if that was possible.

"Are you sure?" he asked softly.

I ignored Zinnia's scowl and pressed a kiss to his lips. "I'm sure. They'll need to know you're all right. We can all meet up again later." If I wasn't so hungry, I would have suggested we turn around right now and leave again. Added to that, the key in my pocket hadn't even given me a slight sign of where the third one was. Without that, we'd fly blind anyway.

As much as I hated the idea, we'd have to bide our time and even humour Zinnia. At least for now.

"Very well." He gave my hand a squeeze and headed for the door.

I watched him leave, then turned back to my sister. "You left my room empty, hmmm?"

She shrugged. "Calla insisted. For some reason

she assumed you would slink back here someday." She rolled her eyes as though the argument had become tiresome a long time ago.

"She was right," I said dryly. Slink? I couldn't decide if I was offended or not. Nor was I sure what to make of Calla sticking up for me. True, she'd always been slightly less of a bitch than Zinnia. Perhaps I underestimated her. If that was true, maybe Zinnia wasn't quite as bad as I remembered.

Zinnia helped me to make up my mind a moment later when she said, "You should all go and bathe. You smell repulsive. Worse than the taint."

"You've been out and had a sniff?" Saff asked, apparently unable to contain himself any further.

"I am queen," she said coldly. "It's my *duty* to know what my subjects are faced with." She gave Huon a meaningful look. "I have been out there several times to assess the progress of the taint."

"Oh, *several* times," Saff said and nodded slowly. "Well I'm sure your subjects are grateful for all of those times." He turned to me and smiled out of the side of his mouth.

Zinnia gave him a look as though she wasn't sure if he was trying to goad her or not.

"And how fast is it spreading?" I asked.

She sniffed. "We will discuss that later, after

you're clean. Although, you really should leave the leading to the leaders, instead of worrying your pretty little head about it."

I thought for a moment she'd pat my cheek. If she tried, she might lose a finger or two. I was in no mood to be patronised further.

I managed a sweet smile. "It's everyone's concern," I said. "We should have some idea how long we have to live."

Her smile faltered and she glanced at Fletcher. The look she gave him sent chills down my spine. It was nothing like the lustful gaze she'd given Kale. No, she wanted more than a bed partner, she wanted power.

The orb felt heavy in my pocket. The key too. Whatever we did, I had to make sure she didn't know about them. The orb in particular might give her what she sought. A way to take our people from the Fae realm to the human realm and establish a new kingdom there.

The last thing anyone needed was to click on their social media and see a new selfie or post from Zinnia, Fae Queen of Earth.

I shuddered to myself. "Right then, bath time. I think we can all fit in the same one." I gave Zinnia a dazzling smile, which left her to gape. Evidently, while she had power, she still wasn't well-liked. I would have to use that to my advantage. Even when we found the key and stopped the taint, we'd have to win back Huon's throne.

No pressure.

"This is bullshit," Huon growled as soon as we were alone in my room. The trolls remained outside, but for now it was just the four of us. "I'm the king. They should all be..." He shook his head. "I never should have gone to the human realm. We knew time moves slower there."

I put my hand on his arm. For a moment he looked as though he might shake it off, but he exhaled and covered my hand with his.

"We didn't know it would move this quickly," I reminded him. "If we had, we could have planned for it."

"I thought we had," he said bitterly. "My mother." He clenched his teeth and his nose twitched like it did when he was trying not to cry. "She was fine when we left."

"When Birch became sick, he went quickly too," I said softly. "Maybe it's the taint. Everything is moving faster than it should."

He ran a hand over his hair. "I know, you're right, but if I had stayed…"

"Then what? You don't know what might have happened. We might have failed to find the second key."

He opened his mouth to reply, but a knock at the door made us both jump.

"Who is it?" I called out, my breath held in the back of my throat.

The door swung open and my other sister, Calla, hurried inside. She closed the door behind her gingerly, as if the sound would draw too much attention.

"Summer, it really is you!" She took the few steps toward me and threw her arms around me.

I stood still in surprise before I hugged her back.

"Shouldn't you be calling me Gardenia?" I asked dryly.

She drew back and gave me a rueful smile. "Don't tell Zinnia."

I snorted softly. "Don't worry, talking to her is the last thing I want to do."

Calla sighed." I know. She's become even worse."

Huon frowned at us both. "When we left, you and her were as thick as thieves. What changed?"

"If anything, "Saff said.

I knitted my brow. "They have a point." I stepped away from her. "How do we know Zinnia didn't send you?"

She pursed her lips.

"Do you have something to hide?" I asked.

"Why are you asking?" Calla sagged a little. "All right, Zinnia and I were always closer than Gard—Summer and I. Zinnia always liked to have someone to agree with her. Summer was always so confident, so beautiful and popular."

I stared at her. "Huh?" Was she talking about me? "Maybe you remember me that way because it's been a couple of years? You know, like when people die and other people only want to remember the good bits."

Behind me, Fletcher let out a choking sound. I turned toward him as he wiped away a tear. I took his hand and drew him toward me. For a moment, he resisted. Then he let me pull him into my arms. "We will get back and find Rick, all right? I promise."

"Who is this Rick?" Calla asked.

I twisted my face enough to say, "Fletcher's brother. "I leaned my head against Fletcher's chest. "It's a long story."

"I have time," she replied.

"We don't," Huon snapped. "If you want to be useful, get us some food."

Calla looked taken aback. Her mouth set in a thin line. "I understand you have no reason to trust me…"

Part of me wanted to reach out to her but I was tired. Tired of this journey and tired of the way she and Zinnia treated me in the past. True she had been the least annoying of my sisters, but still...

"You haven't given me a reason yet," I said.

She flinched. "You may not believe me, but I did try. I told Zinnia to ease up on you. I—" She sniffed.

"You should try to make up with her," Fletcher said softly.

When I looked up at him in surprise, the sides of his mouth drew back.

"You don't know when your time will run out." He exhaled. "I know, we'll go back and find Rick, but your sister is here, right now."

"Yes, and I wouldn't trust her as far as I could throw her," Huon snapped. "How do we know she didn't kill my mother?"

Calla paled. "I would never be a party to murder."

"Maybe Birch didn't get sick," Saff said softly.

"All right, all of you just stop." I stepped away and rubbed my temples. "We need food and a bath. I'm done fighting and thinking about any of this." I turned back around and shook my head.

"Calla, we will talk, but later. When we have some real time." If we did. All of this talk was distracting from what really mattered; the keys and the taint.

I watched her face. She seemed genuinely disappointed. I knew she would report back to Zinnia, whether she wanted to or not. Zinnia would press until Calla told her every word of our conversation. All the more reason not to tell her anything, at least until we had good reason to be sure we could trust her. And, to be fair, vice versa.

"I've arranged for your food to be sent up," Calla said, her expression unreadable. Was that a warning of some kind? If so, it was unnecessary. I would eat everything with great care.

"If you go down to the baths, it should be here when you get back." She eyed all three men speculatively. They returned her look with either hostility or indifference. Fletcher was lost in thought, his face drawn.

I sighed softly to myself. I was no fan of Rick, but

if he was here... I almost snorted at that train of thought. He was good at saying exactly what he thought. He would have given Zinnia a piece of his mind. On one hand, she deserved it, on the other, she could have him tossed off the palace roof.

The gods only knew what she would make of Tiny.

"Maybe the men can start without you," Calla said tentatively. "I really think we should talk."

"You're not going to be alone with Summer," Huon snapped. "If you have something to say, you can say it in front of us."

Saff nodded and did his best to look threatening, but mostly looked as though he needed to fart.

I stifled a laugh and crossed my arms over my chest. "All right, get on with it then."

Calla looked down at her feet. "I've been looking through the libraries. Both of them."

Huon's scowl deepened.

I smirked at him. He hadn't even told me about Birch's secret library until after we'd begun this quest. While I'd forgiven him, I wasn't sure he could condemn anyone else for using it.

"And?" I prompted.

Calla looked up. "I found a reference to the taint."

I blinked. "You *what?*" My gaze flicked to Huon,

but he looked as surprised as I was. "What did it say?"

She licked her lips. "It didn't make much sense," she said.

"Tell us anyway," Huon said.

"It said—" She stopped to think. "The key to the death of the Fae realm lies at the heart."

I exchanged confused looks with the guys. Was the mention of a key a literal reference or a figurative one?

"What else did it say?" Huon asked, his expression guarded.

"Nothing which made sense." Calla took a few steps away and turned. She seemed to enjoy being the centre of attention, even Huon's hostility. It took her a while to respond, making me think she drew it out on purpose.

"Get on with it," Huon snapped. Evidently he assumed the same thing. "Or better yet, show us this book you found."

She bit her lip. "If Zinnia found out I showed you—"

"That will be nothing compared to what will happen if you don't," Huon growled. "Whatever your sister may think, I am king here and I will get back my throne. If you want me to look upon you favourably when that happens, here's your chance to prove yourself."

I saw the wheels turn in Calla's mind as she weighed his words and her current situation, whatever that was. Under Zinnia's thumb, at least. Or on a tight leash. Now I thought about it, she never did anything without Zinnia's input. Our oldest sister had looked over both of our shoulders for as long as I could remember. I gave up paying her any attention long ago. Until now at least, when circumstances gave me no choice.

She reached into the folds of her gown.

I froze.

Huon drew a knife and held it toward her chest.

"Bloody hells," Fletcher muttered.

Calla drew out a book and offered it to Huon. Her eyes were huge and focused on the blade. Her fingers trembled.

He eyed it, then put his knife away slowly. "Next time just say you're going to reach for a book," he warned. "We're all weary and on edge here."

She nodded. "So I noticed." She backed up a few steps, her gaze on him the entire time.

He made an indeterminate grunt and opened the book.

"Which page?" His brow creased. He closed the

book and looked at the leather spine. "Where did this come from? It's not one of Birch's."

"How do you know?" I asked. The book didn't appear to be anything special, apart from being a book.

"I've never seen it before," he replied.

"Can you remember every book you've ever laid a hand on?" Saff asked in disbelief. "You probably can't even remember the name of every woman you've laid a hand on."

Huon cleared his throat. "No, but I would remember one called *The Battle for Dark Magic*," he replied. "I would have chosen it first."

"It sounds like a novel," I said.

He nodded. "Exactly." He paused before he added, "Even though we were looking for a way to bring back lesser magic, I wasn't taking it seriously at the time."

I smirked. "No shit."

He raised a brow. "And you were?"

I snorted. "Of course not, but I might if you hadn't distracted me so often."

"I don't remember hearing you complain about being distracted," he said, amused now. "In fact, I remember you saying, 'Yes, yes yes,' quite a bit."

I flushed. "If we'd focused, we might have found

an answer by now. Which reminds me," I turned to Calla, "you didn't answer his question. Where did that book really come from?"

Calla swallowed. "I might have borrowed it some time ago." She looked toward the floor. "Anything to do with dark magic, I wanted to read."

I gave her a flat stare. "Were you going to try to use dark magic?" I asked.

"I—" her expression went from embarrassment to panic.

I felt sick. "What did you do?"

She licked her lips. "I might have found some spells."

"And?" I pressed.

"And nothing. They required the dark artefacts."

There it was, the admission she knew a lot more about all of this that she'd first let on.

"You tried to find them, didn't you?" Saff asked.

"I studied in the hope of finding their location, yes," she replied. "I was tired of Zinnia always telling me what to do. And you weren't much better." She frowned at me.

I didn't much like her blaming me for anything she might have done, but I pushed my annoyance aside. "Did you find them?"

Calla sighed. "No, just hints as to their where-abouts, and that bit about a key."

"I see," I replied. That was fortunate, although we knew exactly where the artefacts were.

"Have you found the first two keys yet?" Calla asked. Her question caught me by surprise and the answer was written on my face before I could stop it.

"I see you have," she said. "I want to help find the third."

CHAPTER FOUR

"**W**hat do you think?" I asked Huon. "Do you really believe she wants to help?"

He shrugged and ran the soap over my arm. "She's your sister, you tell me."

I sighed and leaned back against the side of the bath. It was more a pond which got fed by a small creek than an actual bath, but Fae of the past had added stones to the sides and heated the water with the use of magic.

Of course that led to other problems. Fae who shared the bath seldom agreed on the temperature, so it frequently rose and fell depending on how long anyone could tolerate being too hot or too cold.

I surreptitiously adjusted it to make it a little

warmer and caught Saff's grimace. The temperature promptly dropped. I raised it again.

"I believe her when she says she's tired of Zinnia," I said slowly, "but the gods only know what Zinnia knows." I kept my words vague for the benefit of the trolls who hovered nearby. Saff suggested they join us, but they had ignored him.

"I don't think she's told anyone," Fletcher said softly. "She seemed genuinely anxious. Not that I know her," he added quickly.

I nodded thoughtfully. "I want to think she's sincere," I said. "In the meantime, maybe we can enjoy this bath." I watched them all through my lashes.

"Good idea." Saff bobbed over and leaned into me. He pressed his erect cock against my leg.

I slipped my hand under the water to grip his length. He thrust in and out of my curled fingers a couple of times, slow and deliberate.

Huon bobbed behind me and ran a hand down my leg, around to my pussy.

I parted my legs. He slid a finger inside me. Apparently no one was in the mood to wait today.

I bent my knee to open myself up further. I expected Huon to slip in another finger, or massage my clit. Instead, he moved around me, put a hand under my leg to hold it, then penetrated me with one firm thrust of his cock.

I groaned out loud at the suddenness of his entrance.

"Sorry," he said into my ear. "I needed to take what was mine." He pulled back and thrust again, harder this time.

"Mine too," Saff said, breathless.

"Mine as well." Fletcher moved to the other side of me and claimed my breasts with his hands.

How had I gotten so lucky? I arched my back and matched Huon's thrusts with bucks.

Saff pressed his lips to mine. His tongue invaded my mouth in the same forceful way Huon's cock had. I parted my lips. He thrust inside, almost in sync with Huon.

I moaned.

Fletcher rolled my nipples with his fingers. He leaned in to suckle one when I pushed my breast out of the water.

Saff broke off the kiss and moved around beside Fletcher. With a cheeky smile, he looked toward Fletcher's erection.

Fletcher's eyes widened in surprise.

"Can I touch you?" Saff asked, suddenly looking anxious.

Fletcher swallowed audibly. "I…um… yes. I've. always wondered how it would feel to…"

"Fuck a guy?" Saff asked with a smile.

Fletcher nodded, his face pink.

"I'm willing if you are." Saff put his hand under the water and curled it around Fletcher's cock. He stroked it a time or two, his eyes on Fletcher's face and parted lips.

"We can go further if you want to?" Saff said softly. "I'd like to, but no pressure." He reached for a bottle beside the bath and offered it to him.

Typical of Fae to leave lubricant for anyone who needed it.

Fletcher blinked a few times. His face was red by now, but desire filled his gaze. "I'd like that," he replied, his voice slightly choked.

Saff stroked his cock another time or two, then slowly, deliberately, turned around. He braced himself against the wall beside me.

By now, I was so aroused I could barely see straight. Watching Fletcher grip Saff's hip with one hand and put his cock into position against his ass, drove me almost to the edge.

"Are you sure?" Fletcher asked.

"Very sure," Saff replied. "If you are. Don't let me rush you if you're not ready."

"I'm ready," Fletcher said softly. "So ready..." He prepared Saff quickly, then oh so slowly sank his cock into Saff's ass.

Saff's eyes closed. He looked ecstatic.

Fletcher sighed softly, a sound of pure bliss.

Huon groaned. "Fuck, that's hot," he said with a grunt. With one hand on me, he rubbed the other up and down Saff's cock.

"I could get used to all this sharing," Saff said, his voice husky. "We should invite Kale some time."

I murmured my agreement. Even surrounded by three guys, I wanted to know how his hands felt on me. Would he touch the other guys like this? None of us would pressure him, but the gods knew I never had so much fun in this bath.

Fletcher's eyes were closed and his breathing was ragged. "Gods, I had no idea."

Saff grinned. "I know, I'm awesome, aren't I?"

Huon chuckled and pulled out of me. "They gave me an idea." He turned me around and pressed me against the side of the bath. He pried my ass cheeks apart and I felt his cook prod against my back entrance.

"I'm going to fuck your ass," he said into my ear.

"Mmm, yes." I wanted him to fill me, whatever hole he chose.

Even with the water, and lubricant, he pressed into me slowly, giving me time to stretch bit by bit more to take him in.

"Gods, yes," he murmured. He pushed himself in deeper. Him filling me like that was pure, perfect ecstasy. Pleasure and pain at the same time.

He reached around to run his hands over my breasts and down to my clit. He ran his fingertips over it slowly as he thrust into my ass.

I was back on the edge of the precipice in a matter of moments.

"Oh, gods." Fletcher cried out. I turned my head in time to see his face clenched in concentration and bliss. His body slapped against Saff's with each frantic thrust before he came inside Saff.

"Please…" That was the only word I could manage.

"Come," was all Huon said in reply.

Fletcher coming had thrown Huon and I both over the edge. I was swept away in a tsunami, dragged down in its force. I didn't bother trying to hold back a cry.

Huon grunted in my ear and thrust so hard it hurt, but heightened my orgasm. My head spun faster than when we were in the portal, but this time with pure pleasure. This was a place I could happily get lost in.

As I was coming down, Huon sagged against me. He pulled out as Saff drew away from Fletcher.

Saff smiled and turned me around. Without a word, he picked me up, wound my legs around his waist and pushed his cock into my hot, wet pussy. He pressed me back against the side of the bath and thrust with hasty blows of pent up lust.

He only took a few moments, a dozen heartbeats of pounding into me. He let out a long, ragged grunt and came inside me, spilling his cum into my body, and into the water.

"Gods and all the seven hells," he said as he sagged between my legs. "That was incredible."

I smiled. "I guess we're all feeling our mortality today." I never had a lover take me like that before. Or each other for that matter. It felt as though they all knew what they wanted and hadn't hesitated to claim it. To claim me. And Fletcher had tried something I suspected he'd never done before. Damn, just thinking about that made me hot again.

Saff let me down and I reclined against the side of the bath and embraced the languid feeling which washed over me.

Huon slipped in beside me and drew me into his arms. He kissed my neck lightly.

"Marry me," he said softly.

I blinked shook my head slightly. "I beg your pardon?"

He smiled. "I said, marry me."

Beside him, Saff pouted.

Huon waved a hand at him. "Marry him too, if you like. My mother had three husbands and it didn't do them or her any harm. Well, mostly." He sighed sadly. "Two died long before my father." He nodded toward Fletcher. "One was human. The other was reckless."

Saff perked up. "Right. You could marry all of us. Kale too if you want."

"I—" I hesitated and frowned. "Is this about us feeling our mortality? If that's the only reason—"

"It's not," Huon said firmly. "It's because I love you and want you to be my queen."

"And I love you and want you to be his queen," Saff said with a grin. "We make a good team, especially in the bath." He winked at Fletcher, who blushed.

I raised my eyebrows at Fletcher.

"I love you," he said, "but I can't think about things like this until I know my brother is all right."

I ran a hand over my hair and rang out a handful. "Fletcher is right, now isn't the time to think about this." I pressed a finger to Huon's lips. "When this is over, ask me again, all right?"

"I will, if you promise to say yes," he replied.

"I promise," I said slowly, "to think about it."

Huon grimaced, but drew me in for a soft kiss. "Deal. I'll respect whatever you decide."

I snorted. "The hells you will. You'll ask again and again until I say yes."

He grinned. "So say yes straight away. Or I could insist."

"I'll bear than in mind." I leaned back and looked toward our troll guards through slitted eyes. Their faces were expressionless, but the two males had tented pants which spoke volumes. They weren't so different from us Fae. We had a common ancestor, after all. I wondered what they were like as lovers. Could we breed with trolls? I saw no reason why not, but the gods only knew if any offspring would have wings or not.

"Wondering what it would be like to screw a troll?" Saff asked, his voice low.

I gave him a sidelong look. "I was thinking our two people should come together, for the good of both races."

"Coming together is something I'm always in favour of," Huon remarked. "Sexually and otherwise. When I get my throne back, I'll make peace between everyone in the Fae realm."

"Except screamspinners," Saff said.

"Except them," Huon agreed. "They're on their own."

"What about mimicats?" I asked.

"We should learn more about them," Huon said. "And maybe suggest trolls stop eating them."

I glanced back toward the trolls. One watched me with unreadable eyes. If he was anything like Tavar, he would be clever, but hard to read and with little to no sense of humour. Trolls valued honour over frivolities like jokes. Personally, I thought laughter made even the worst situation more bearable, but I knew not everyone saw life the same way I did. That was probably fortunate. If everyone was like me, the realms were doomed.

At least they wouldn't be boring.

"I think the mimicats would appreciate that," I agreed. "Maybe they can eat screamspinners instead."

The troll made a disgusted face. So he was listening.

"What's wrong with eating them?" I called out.

For a moment I thought he'd turn away, but his

eyes narrowed and he said, "Screamspinners are vermin. And they make the tongue go numb."

His companions frowned at him, but he was unperturbed.

"Numb?" I repeated. "That doesn't sound good. How do they taste?"

"Their crunch is pleasant, but their flavour is bitter," he replied. "Mimicat is tastier."

"So is Fae," one of the female trolls said darkly.

The male rounded on her. "If the queen hears you say that..." He turned around and stared at us in alarm.

I put up my hands. "We won't say a thing to her, promise. But—please don't eat Fae."

"Unless it's the right kind of eating," Fletcher said, his voice low.

"Five," I told him, "since they're talking about putting Fae on a plate."

"That's fair," he replied. "I wonder if they eat humans."

"We do not eat humans or Fae," the male replied, his voice tight. "It's a—what do you call those?" He looked thoughtful.

"A joke?" Saff suggested. "What do you know, trolls have a sense of humour after all."

"How about that," I agreed. "I'm not sure I find it funny, but it's a start."

The troll stepped closer and crouched down beside the water. "You really mean to bring our peoples together?" he asked. He made no effort to hide his appraisal of my body. Since female trolls rarely covered their breasts, I decided it wasn't a big deal.

"That's my intention," Huon replied. "We've kept each other at arm's length for long enough. Don't you think?"

The troll nodded. "I think if you say what you mean, we can be allies."

"What's your name?" I asked.

He flinched. "Troll," he replied.

I scowled. "Not what Zinnia calls you. What is your actual name?"

"Daffin," he muttered.

"All right, Daffin," I said. My eyes flicked toward the other trolls. "How loyal are they?"

He raised his chin. "They are very loyal to me. Where I go, they will follow. What I do, they will do. What I say—" He cocked his head. "You understand?"

"Yes, we do." He was so earnest, I could guess how he felt about being under Zinnia's heel. "What about the other trolls?"

He drew back, eyes wide. "I don't know anything about the others," he said quickly. He looked so alarmed I thought he might change his mind about working with us.

"You work in autonomous teams," Huon said, "but under the command of another troll, right?"

"Yes," Daffin replied, his expression wary.

"And you don't interfere with each other?" Huon guessed. "Or talk to other teams about what they're doing?"

"It's considered offensive to pry," Daffin said.

"That might be something you need to work on," Huon said. "If we're going to work together, then we all need to communicate."

Daffin looked as though he'd rather stab himself in the eyeball than go against the way trolls traditionally operated, but I sensed he understood.

"I cannot make any promises," he said slowly, "but I will try."

"Good man." Huon smiled and gave him a curt nod.

"You should probably keep playing along with Zinnia," I said. "Looking friendly with us might put you all under suspicion."

Daffin's mouth drew back. "The last of the trolls

who went against her were exiled. Except their leader. She was executed."

I gasped. That was monstrous. He was risking a lot speaking to us. How low my sister had sunk. Lower than I would have ever suspected. She was much more ruthless than I had given her credit for. That was definitely concerning. We would have to watch ourselves.

"I'll make sure that doesn't happen to you," Huon assured him. "Whatever it takes."

Daffin pressed his fists together and gave a nod. "This is my team's salute. It's a sign of respect."

Huon solemnly returned the salute. After a moment, I did the same.

Allied with trolls against Fae. The realm certainly had changed.

expected Zinnia to put on a lavish feast for us, just to prove she could. The small meal of salad and bread suggested she couldn't. She watched me from the other end of the table as though she expected me to comment. I might have made a snide remark about the lack of food, just to irritate her, but nothing about it was funny.

The less usable land the realm had, the sooner we would all starve.

"So, we were going to discuss the progress of the taint," Huon said bluntly. Clean and in fresh clothes, he looked more like a leader than I had ever seen him.

More like one than Zinnia. She thought so too, I saw that on her face, but I saw something calculating as well. Her thoughts were so transparent I almost laughed aloud.

If she thought Huon would get together with her, to legitimise her claim to the throne, she would have to think again.

Her eyes narrowed. "I'd like to know more about the human realm," she declared. "Let us discuss that first."

"The human realm is a complicated matter," Huon said. "The taint is a simple question."

"The answer isn't so simple," she snapped. "It's—" She stopped short when Kale slipped into the dining room.

He gave her a nod and moved to slip into the seat beside me.

"My apologies for being late," he said.

"Is everything all right?" I whispered.

He regarded me with sad, dark eyes and said, "For the most part, yes. My family is here and... alive."

There was obviously more to that story, but I wouldn't push the issue. Until later. For now, I had to be content to lean against him and inhale the smell of soap and clean cotton.

"Zinnia, sorry, *Queen* Zinnia, was just about to

tell us how fast the taint is spreading," Huon said for Kale's benefit.

"Ah," Kale replied. "Good. I would like to know that myself."

All eyes turned toward Zinnia.

Boxed in, her face turned pink. Anger flashed in her eyes. She looked as though she was thinking furiously about how to turn the conversation in the direction she wanted.

Finally, and with gritted teeth, she replied. "It's spread approximately two hundred kilometres in the last year. Or so my advisors have told me." Naturally, she'd find a way to put any potential blame onto someone else.

"That only gives the capital a matter of weeks," Saff blurted.

Zinnia scowl turned to an expression of real fear. "Yes, it does. Perhaps now you understand the need to discuss the human realm."

"The veil is closed," I reminded her. "We can't travel there."

"And yet, you claim to have done just that," she reminded me. "Unless you lied?"

"No, we didn't lie," Huon said. "We opened a portal which is, in all likelihood, closed now."

"How convenient," she said darkly.

"Not especially," he replied. "But I wouldn't recommend it in any case. It was a wild ride and dumped us in separate places." He explained how we had to find each other again.

"If there is one portal," she said slowly, "there must be other portals."

I looked down at the table, but felt someone's eyes on me. When I raised my head, I caught Calla watching me from across the table. Her expression gave away nothing. For all I knew, she was aware of the orb in my pocket. Gods, she might even know more than me about what it did. Sure, I made it work to bring us here, but that was an accident.

I returned my attention to Zinnia as Huon spoke.

"There might be other portals," he agreed, "but unless one jumps out at us, I don't know how to find it."

"Perhaps your role could be to look," Calla said suddenly. She gestured to us all with one hand. "Think about it. Our time is limited. We have to find a way to leave the realm or we'll die. Someone should be looking around the realm for a way out. Wouldn't you agree, Zinnia?" She smiled sweetly.

I saw the wheels of thought turn in Zinnia's mind. She could, potentially, find a way to the human realm and get rid of Huon at the same time.

She also knew there must be a catch, but she couldn't immediately see one. She regarded us all, one after the other and finally nodded.

"Very well. Consider yourself appointed to look for portals. Your friend Saff can go with you."

"Fine with me," Saff said with a one-shouldered shrug.

"I'm going too," I said, in case there was any doubt in anyone's mind.

Zinnia frowned. I thought she might refuse and provoke an argument I had no intention of losing. Finally, she nodded.

"Fine, Gardenia is permitted to go too. You may take the human with you." She curled her lip and didn't look toward Fletcher.

I did though. He frowned at Zinnia, but looked as though he'd be more than happy to be away from here. He saw me watching and gave me a tiny smile. I responded with a wry one.

"What about Kale?" Calla asked, "Is he coming with us?"

My head whipped around. "Us?" I echoed. "What do you mean us? You're not coming too."

Calla looked smug, for some reason I couldn't grasp. "Of course I am," Calla said. "You don't think Zinnia would let you go without someone to watch over you, do you?" She shook her head. "After all, you might return to the human realm and leave us all to perish."

I rolled my eyes at her dramatic turn of phrase.

Huon spoke before I was able to. "As tempting as that might be," he said coolly, "we have no intention of leaving thousands of Fae to die." He didn't add, "What sort of king would I be?" but I saw it on his face.

Zinnia gave him a scowl, which suggested she knew it too. "You don't seem to mind screwing in the bath when the realm is in dire trouble," she pointed out, her tone as cold as ice.

If she thought she'd shame Huon, she was wrong. He threw back his head and laughed.

"Everyone needs to take a break from time to time, even us."

I agreed with him, but how had she known? Had Daffin told her or was his team less trustworthy than he thought?

Saff's mouth twitched as if he wanted to say something, but held back. Given how outspoken and easygoing he usually was, keeping quiet for this long must be difficult. I knew he didn't like overbearing people any more than I did, but there was more. Something in the way he held his shoulders suggested he was troubled. The gods knew we all had plenty of reason to feel that way, but this was something specific. Something bad.

"It's settled then," Calla said, "we'll leave in the morning."

"I don't recall agreeing to let you come," Huon told her.

"Nor have I agreed to let you go," Zinnia said. She looked down her nose at all of us for a long moment. "However, as Calla pointed out, I'm not sure you can be trusted. Therefore, she will go and a contingent of trolls as well." She pursed her lips. "Furthermore, one of you will remain behind as surety." Her eyes slid to Kale.

"No," I said firmly. "Kale knows more about the realm outside the capital than any one."

"Except the trolls," Zinnia replied. "This is the deal. Take it or doom the realm and all the Fae to die."

Oh, good, she was putting the futures of everyone on my shoulders. And why? Because of her misplaced desire for Kale. If she really thought he'd return the sentiment, she was mistaken.

"If you put everyone at risk because of some game—" Huon's face was pink, his eyes laced with anger and frustration.

Kale interrupted. "I'll stay," he said. He sat around to face me. "You *will* find what you need. I have every faith in you and the others." He gave me a meaningful look which I couldn't interpret.

"What if we don't? "I asked bluntly. "What if we need you?" And the first key. The third might not respond to only one other.

"Then you will know where to find me." He ran the back of his hand across my cheek. "Perhaps I can be of more use here."

I frowned. "I doubt that," I muttered. What was it with everyone today? Everyone had agendas and things they were trying to tell me without speaking in front of Zinnia. I understood the need to keep secrets, but it got on my nerves. Those were drawn tight enough as it was.

I shrugged. "Fine, whatever. You stay here and we'll go and save the realm."

The corners of Kale's mouth twitched upward and I knew he didn't take my fit of annoyance too seriously. "We all have our part to play," he said. There it was again, him being cryptic. This, at least, I understood. He suspected Huon or Saff might be the third foretold. It could even be Fletcher for all we knew.

I sighed. "All right, I supposed it's decided then.

We'll go, find a portal and then come back and round up everyone to evacuate. Zinnia, I assume you will have everyone prepared?"

She shifted in her chair and drew herself up. "I will do my duty as queen," she replied stiffly. I would bet the realm she had her own bags packed already.

"Good." I gave her an insincere smile and looked away as though she was dismissed. She spluttered but said nothing.

I caught the grin on Saff's face but he quashed it before anyone else could see.

He was certainly acting strangely. More so than usual.

"Well then." Huon rose. "It seems we've done all the talking we can. We should get some rest. Kale, I'd like a few words with you before we turn in."

"Of course." Kale rose and I was a step behind.

"We'll see your first thing in the morning," I said to Calla. I waited a moment and hoped she'd say she changed her mind.

She just smiled and nodded. "I'll be ready, " she said cheerfully.

"Right, of course you will." I gave Zinnia a glance before I followed the guys out the door.

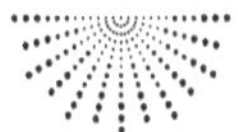

CHAPTER SIX

"All right." I pressed my hands to my hips. "Who wants to start?"

They all looked at each other, then back to me. Huon looked amused. I eyed him for a moment longer. If he wanted a queen, he might just get one. The attitude anyway.

"Kale, Saff, we should start with one of you." I glanced from one to the other.

Huon raised an eyebrow at them.

Fletcher flopped down onto one of the beds to watch. He looked drawn. No doubt I did as well. When this was over, I would sleep for a week or two at least.

Kale pulled over a chair and sat. "I opted to stay because I believe someone should keep an eye on

Zinnia," he explained. "And because she gave us no choice."

"There's always a choice, but it's probably a good idea not to leave her unattended," Huon agreed. He made a face as though he'd tasted something sour. This was not the homecoming any of us expected. "Although," he added, "I hope to hells we aren't away for another five years."

I murmured my agreement, but said, "There wouldn't be much point in returning if we were." I exhaled through my nose and said to Kale, "I really don't like the idea of leaving you alone here."

"Here?" Saff asked "Or with her?" I assumed he was joking, but his mouth was set in a line, no hint of a smile.

"Either of those things," I replied. "You saw how she looked at him." I jerked my head toward the dark skinned Fae.

Kale rose, took my hand and held it to his cheek. "I barely noticed she existed," he rumbled.

I smiled and ran my fingertips over the stubble on his face. It was prickly and tickled, but made him look unbelievably hot. One of these days—

Huon interrupted my thoughts. "Oh, she exists all right," he said bitterly.

My desire deflated. I lowered my hand.

Before I could say anything, Fletcher spoke. "If she hadn't taken the throne, someone else would have," he pointed out.

I nodded slowly. "It could have been Calla, or the gods know who else." I wrinkled my nose. Any number of Fae would have been happy to step into Huon's shoes.

"Calla doesn't seem so bad, " Fletcher said. "As siblings go." A shadow passed over his eyes.

"She's the better of the two of them," I said. "Apart from the whole *looking for dark magic objects* thing."

"Apart from that," Fletcher agreed.

I lowered myself to the bed beside Fletcher and leaned against him as he put an arm around me. I closed my eyes and exhaled. For a moment, I pushed all the trouble out of my mind and pretended my life was just me and my men, not all the danger and drama of the last few days.

The illusion lasted approximately eight seconds before it was shattered again.

"So, when is anyone else going to bring up the fact that Zinnia is probably Myrta?" Saff blurted.

My eyes shot open. I looked up at him in shock.

"I beg your pardon?" I asked. Both my head and my heart started to race. The implications made me beyond nauseous. We all knew Myrta could be anywhere, and inside anyone, but I'd almost convinced myself we left her in the human realm. She couldn't do much damage there, with no magic, and she couldn't get her hands on the keys.

It hadn't even crossed my mind she might have entered the portal with us, much less inhabited the mind and body of my sister. I was no fan of Zinnia but I wouldn't wish being locked in their own body on anyone.

I shook my head. Zinnia seized the throne some years ago, in Fae time. Or had that been Myrta? Had she killed Huon's mother and lain in wait all that time? It made some sense, and yet—

"How?" I asked.

He hesitated, then shrugged. "I don't know how. Magic, I suppose. The portal might have spat her out here. That's possible, right?"

"I suppose so," I agreed tentatively.

"Maybe she found another portal, or got to the orb first." Saff was just throwing out theories now, but that didn't mean he was wrong. "You saw how Khat reacted to her. I didn't believe him the first time, I won't make that mistake again." He gave me an apologetic look, but I waved it off. That was the past and there was no point in dwelling on it.

"Khat certainly took a dislike to her. But then, he

doesn't seem to like anyone." I rubbed my forehead with my fingertips. "He didn't say anything before he took off. Apart from hissing at her, he gave no sign."

"He's Khat," Huon said, "he probably assumed a hiss was all we needed."

"That's true," I conceded. "If we didn't understand, it was all our fault." I rolled my eyes, then frowned. "If Zinnia is Myrta, that means she also knows about the keys. She's sending us to look for them for her." While keeping Kale and the first key close to her. "Do you think Calla knows?"

"She didn't seem to," Saff said thoughtfully, "but nothing would surprise me at this point."

"Me either," I agreed. I lay back and looked up at the ceiling. "Should I try to blast Myrta out of her? Zinnia is a pain, but she doesn't deserve to have Myrta in her head."

"Myrta would just go somewhere else," Fletcher said. "At least this way we know where she is and Kale can keep an eye on her."

I groaned. "All the more reason I don't like the idea of him staying here." I picked up my head.

"That brings us to what I wanted to talk to Kale about." Huon sat beside me and made the bed dip. "I need you to look through the library for references to the taint, the keys, anything. Now we have a better idea of what to look for, you might be able to find something I didn't."

Kale inclined his head. "Of course. I will get straight into doing so."

"Try not to look too obvious," Huon added.

"If asked, I will tell Zinnia I'm looking for reference to a portal. She couldn't want me to stop doing that."

"Myrta might, but as Zinnia, she won't have an excuse to tell you to stop," Saff said.

"Indeed," Kale agreed.

"Furthermore," Huon continued, "I need you to make sure the Fae really are ready to leave if they have to. Zinnia might do her duty," he smirked, "but Myrta won't care. In fact, she'll be only too happy to leave everyone here to die. I won't allow that."

"Of course you won't." I rolled over and looked him in the eyes. "But it won't be necessary. We'll find that last key and release lesser magic back into the realm."

"I like your optimism, but we have to be realistic. If we can't find the last key in time, we have to plan for a contingency. If that means we use the orb to take us all to the human realm, then so be it."

"That's only a temporary fix," Fletcher said. "Especially when humans discover Fae living amongst them. We're not good at dealing with those who are a little different." He lightly touched the scars on his face.

"And we're a *lot* different," Saff said. "Although it's not hard to hide our wings if we want to. We can't hide our awesomeness as easily though." He grinned. Now this was the Saff I knew and loved.

I laughed and sat up. "That's true, but I'm sure we can suppress it if we have to. We can't pretend we don't live longer though."

My gaze flicked to Fletcher. Unless the hunt for the last key killed one of us, he would be the first to age and die naturally. I hated to think of it. I would adore him no matter how old he was, but for us to look young while he got older—that seemed so unfair.

"Let's worry about that when it becomes a problem," Huon said. "At the moment we need to focus on the tasks at hand." He counted them off on his fingers. "Find the last key, prepare the Fae, stay alive."

"Is that in order?" Saff asked. "I would have put the last one first. It seems kinda important."

Huon looked thoughtful. "You're right. Let's bump that up to the top of the list."

Saff nodded, satisfied. "Top priority, check."

I cocked my head at him. "Hey, Saff, do you have

any family here?" I knew he and Huon had known each other for a long time, but that was really all I knew.

He tweaked his nose. "I have parents and several siblings. They're probably in the capital, but my place is here."

"Saff's family call him Saffy and treat him like he's three," Huon said helpfully.

"Thanks, buddy," Saff said sarcastically and grimaced at him. "I was hoping to avoid sharing that information with everyone."

"Saffy?" I tried to suppress a grin, but it broke out, regardless. "It could be worse, it could be Saffy-poo."

Saff turned red. "They might call me that too," he muttered.

I couldn't help myself, I laughed. "Suddenly Gardenia doesn't seem so bad."

"Should we call you Saffy-poo?" Fletcher asked teasingly.

"Only if you want us to call you Fletchy-poo," Saff retorted. He stuck his tongue out at Fletcher.

"I think I'll pass," Fletcher replied. "But thanks anyway."

"I'm curious." I leaned my shoulder against his. "What were you called as a child?"

Fletcher leaned his head until it touched mine.

"Just Fletch. The kids at school used to call me Fletcho or Remo. Aussies like to put an O at the end of things as a nickname. You'd be Summo." He smiled. "Kaleo, Saffo. Huon wouldn't really work."

"Hu-o," I suggested.

"It doesn't exactly roll off the tongue," Huon said.

"You might have to be Huey then," Fletcher said. "There you go, you're ready to be Australians if you have to."

I chuckled. "I'm not sure I'm ready to be Summo, but whatever it takes to fit in." I hoped to gods it wasn't necessary.

"We should get some sleep," Huon said. "Saffo, Kale-o, I think there's room on this bed for you two too."

"Right-o, Huey," Saff said smartly. "Or is that King Huey?"

"Huon is fine," Huon said. "You can call me king when I get my throne back."

Saff paused. "You know I'm not really calling you king, no matter what happens, right?"

"I suspected you might not," Huon agreed. "Young Fae these days, they have no respect." He sighed dramatically.

I laughed softly. "I'd sooner respect you than Queen Zinnia. Or Queen Myrta. That begs the question though." The smile faded from my face. "How long will it take before Zinnia is gone and Myrta is all that's left inside her?"

As I suspected, no one had an answer for that. It was just another reason why we needed to hurry up and find the last key. With a lot of luck, we might even save Zinnia, along with the rest of the realm.

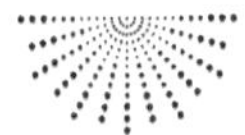

CHAPTER SEVEN

"I don't suppose anyone has looked into where the centre of the taint is?" Huon asked. He fixed Calla with a look which suggested he wished she would stay behind.

"I don't suppose they have," Calla agreed. "Zinnia didn't want anyone to go near it, and what could I do?"

"You could have gone yourself and looked," I said flatly. "That's what I would have done."

"Yes, you would," she agreed. "You're impetuous and headstrong. I, on the other hand, am cautious. I searched the libraries for information rather than rushing off half-cocked."

"If there's anything Summer has, it's cocks," Saff said. "Well, not one of her own, but... you know."

"Maybe you should quit while you're ahead?" I suggested.

He rubbed his chin thoughtfully. "I think you're right. Still, half-cocked isn't accurate, so—" He threw his hands up when I ached my eyebrows at him. "All right, all right, I surrender."

"Good." I nodded. "So we've established that no Fae have gone to look for where the taint began."

"No Fae," Huon agreed. "What about trolls or mimicats?"

"Good point." I waved Daffin over.

He eyed Calla with carefully disguised mistrust.

"Daffin, do you know if any trolls have explored the taint?" I asked.

A flash of surprise crossed his face. "I would think so," he agreed. "Korta's contingent spent some time in the area."

"Korta," I repeated. "Tavar's commander?"

"I believe so," he agreed. "I requested Tavar's presence on my team. With your permission, she'll join us." His eyes flicked uncertainly from me, to Huon, to Calla and back again.

"Yes, she has my permission." I manage to contain my delight at having her along again. I trusted her implicitly. "She was useful in the past."

"I agree," Huon said, his expression also guarded. "She can come."

Calla cleared her throat. "I am acting on behalf of her highness."

"And Summer and I are in charge of this mission," Huon said coldly. "If you don't like it, you can stay here." He turned his back before she could reply and took his pack from Saff's hands.

"It seems that's decided," I said. "Thank you, Daffin. I appreciate your initiative."

The troll almost beamed at my praise. I had never seen that much emotion from a troll. It was fascinating.

Beside me, Huon cleared his throat. "Daffin, can you round up your team and make sure they're ready to leave?"

"Yes, sir," Daffin replied smartly and hurried away.

"I think he has a crush on you," Huon told me.

Calla looked horrified.

I just smiled. "He has good taste, obviously." I puffed my chest out and gave Huon a wink.

He chuckled. "You're right, he does." He kissed my mouth and snaked an arm around my waist.

Calla's face turned pink and she looked about ready to pop. I knew what she must be thinking;

why would all these men be interested in me? The gods only knew how often I wondered that myself. As far as I was concerned, I was nothing special, just Summer, the Fae who could blow things up.

My gaze wandered to Fletcher, who had been quiet all morning. I also knew what he was thinking. The longer this took, the longer it would be until we returned to the human realm. As much as I hated to dismiss—well, not his anxiety, but the reason for it— Rick couldn't be a priority right now. Nor could Yina, the Seafae. Even Jude, who deserved to be sucked into all of this even less than Rick, had to be pushed to the back of my mind.

"He'll be all right," Huon said into my ear. "He's strong. Remember what he survived before you met him?"

"I know," I whispered back. Stuck alone in the dark, in a strange place, for months on end. The fact he hadn't lost his mind was miraculous, especially so close to the dark magic artefacts and the room they were locked away in. If I had known they were there when I was so close to them, I might have freaked out a lot more than I had. I couldn't discount the idea that the artefacts had some kind of impact on both of us, but I had yet to see any sign of it.

"I just wish we knew everything would turn out the way we hope," I added.

"It will," he assured me. "We're badasses, remember? We've survived for this long, we can finish it. Besides, the ancients wanted us to succeed. Everything they set up was for us. Puzzles for us to solve, challenges for us to overcome."

"Stress for us to deal with," I said cynically.

"I think that goes with the territory," he said wryly.

"Oh?" I asked. "What territory is that?"

"Being a hero," he replied with a smile.

"I wouldn't call myself that," I said. "If I'd known what Birch was getting us into, I would have said no and spent the rest of the week in bed."

He snorted a laugh and blew warm air on my earlobe. "No, you wouldn't. You could never resist a challenge. That's why we work so well, you and I."

"Because you're a challenge?" I teased. "That's one word for you. Pain in the ass being another."

"That's three words," he pointed out.

I socked him on the arm. While he rubbed it, I nodded toward Tavar, who appeared with her bag on her back. She also looked clean, but her face was the usual guarded mask, maybe even more so than when I'd seen her last.

"Tavar," I greeted her warmly. "I'm glad you're coming with us."

"Summer," she replied. "My duty is with my people and the task at hand, as always."

"I think that's Tavar-speak for, 'Hells yeah, bitches, let's get going,'" Huon said.

She gave a quirk of a brow. "We should make haste," she replied.

I held back a smile. It wasn't quite what Huon suggested, but I knew she too wanted to head out. "All right then, Fletcher, who do you want to travel with?"

He looked from me to Saff and back again.

The red-haired Fae smiled. "Come with me," he said and gave Fletcher a wink.

Fletcher blushed. He glanced back at me.

"I should fly with Tavar," I told him. "She has more idea of where we need to go than anyone." I wasn't sure she and Huon trusted each other enough yet, so I was the logical choice.

Fletcher nodded. "That makes sense."

"Don't worry," Saff told him, "I'll keep my hands to myself." He rubbed them together.

"Just don't drop me," Fletcher said. "That's a dick move I don't need." He smiled at me.

I thought for a moment. "I think it gets a nine," I said finally.

"I agree," Saff said with a warm smile.

Fletcher fist pumped the air and stood still while Saff shrunk him and picked him up.

"Cute," Saff said. "You'll fit in all sorts of interesting places." He tucked Fletcher into a pocket. He caught my look and feigned innocence. "What? I said I'd keep my hands to myself. I didn't say anything about my imagination. That wanders around at will. I have no control over it." He gestured with both hands, palms outward.

"That doesn't surprise me," I replied. My imagination was pretty wild at times too. I certainly couldn't point too many fingers at others.

"Life is too short not to use your imagination wherever possible," Huon said. "And act on it once in a while." He wiggled his brows.

I nodded and was about to say something when Khat rubbed past my legs.

"Who am I flying with?" he asked.

"How nice of you to grace us with your presence," Huon said dryly.

"I know, right?" Khat said. "I woke up this morning feeling magnanimous, and here I am."

I snorted a laugh. "We're honoured you would deign to come back."

"You should be," Khat replied. "Also, the mimicats have moved closer to the capital, so I've found them, spoken to the council and now I'm here to share my wisdom."

"Good," I nodded. "Maybe you can travel with Huon?" I looked at him questioningly. Over his shoulder, I saw Calla scowl at Khat. Her lip curled in disgust, which lasted a matter of moments before she forced her mouth in a neutral line.

I probably had that same look on my face when I first met Khat. That was another thing we needed to work on. Mimicats were ornery—at least Khat was —but they were as harmless as trolls and at least as smart.

"I think I can stand to travel with him," Khat said in my voice. "As long as he doesn't squash me."

Huon grinned. "I'll try not to."

Khat's tail flicked back and forth. "Try hard. I still bite. Where is Kale?"

"He's staying here," I told him.

"I see," Khat said in Kale's voice. "Excellent. I quite like mimicking him. Perhaps I shall talk like this for the rest of the journey. That would be good indeed."

"How about you don't?" I said. "Is your usual

voice yours?" I had wondered that since we met, but it seemed rude to ask.

"Who else's voice would it be?" Khat reverted back to the one I was used to.

"Someone you had for lunch?" Saff suggested.

"I'll have *you* for lunch," Khat said in Saff's voice. "I'll have you know, I don't eat Fae…anymore. Unless it's a choice between that and starving to death. I'm nice, not stupid."

I opened my mouth to question whether or not he was actually nice, but thought better of it. We needed our allies right now, all of them. "All right then, Huon can put you on his shoulder and we'll get going."

Calla moved to grab my arm and pulled me aside. "Are we really bringing that cat along?"

"He's a member of our team," I told her. "He's been quite valuable in the past."

Khat, apparently having heard the exchange, hissed in Calla's direction. "Do we need to bring her?" he asked. "She smells funny."

I blinked. "Funny as in humorous or funny as in strange?"

"Funny as in shady as fuck," Khat replied. "She's up to something."

Calla scowled and bared her teeth at him. "I'm

helping save the realm from certain death, and being eaten by mimicats," she snapped.

"All right, all right." I held my hands up between them. "You two will have to learn to get along. Calla, Khat has helped us a lot. Khat, Calla is my sister."

"Are you sure about that?" He sniffed in her direction.

I frowned. "Yes, of course I am. Can we please stop wasting time? The sooner we go, the sooner we can save the realm." His unease made my skin tingle, but I pushed it aside for now.

I looked toward Saff, whose gaze swung from Calla to Khat and back again. His expression was guarded, his brow creased slightly.

I knew he was determined to listen to Khat's instincts, but I was sure his concern was misplaced this time. Calla might have some kind of agenda, but she was still my sister. Whatever she might be up to, I could manage her.

I hoped.

"Yes, let's get going. Daffin and his trolls can each travel with one of us." Huon scooped Khat up before he could say another word. He snaked his arm around the closest troll and spread his wings.

I put an arm around Tavar and another around

Daffin and followed them. Daffin's eyes were huge as we soared over the treetops.

We were a strange group, that was for sure.

I glanced back to where Kale stood alone on the top of the palace. I gave him a nod, which he responded to with a raise of his hand in the air. A moment later, he was out of sight and a heavy feeling settled into the bottom of my stomach.

CHAPTER EIGHT

*D*eep within the land close to where the taint began, the trees and plants no longer smelt like death. Once, they must have, a hint of the smell lingered in the air, but the vegetation had long since withered and died. All that remained were dried husks and patches of black where fire had swept through. The breeze blew dust across the top layer of dirt, which was packed too hard for anything to grow.

I kicked at a blackened stump with the toe of my boot. It crumbled and fell apart.

"The ground here is so hard, I can't even kick it up over my own pee," Khat complained.

"That's right near the bottom of my list of things

I'm worried about," I told him. "At the top is the fact there's nothing here."

"Right," Fletcher agreed. "Just dirt, dust and death."

"And no sign of anywhere for a key to hide," I said. The one in my pocket was acting remarkably like an ordinary key. In no way did it pull me anywhere or give any indication of which way it wanted us to go.

"Can anyone feel anything?" I asked. "Anything at all?"

"No." Huon looked troubled.

"Just you," Saff replied. "The bond I have with you feels stronger here."

I looked down at myself. "Maybe I'm a key."

"You don't look like a key," Saff said.

"I don't feel like one either," I said. "If I was supposed to bond with the keys and turn into one, I guess it would have happened by now?"

"That seems logical," Huon said. He rubbed his chin. "If everything we've seen and done so far is an indication, that bond of Saff's is there for a reason. Saff, can you hold Summer's hand and see if something happens?"

"Gladly." He took my hand and, for good measure, leaned in for a kiss.

My skin tingled where his fingers touched, and when our lips met, but that was all.

"I don't feel anything different," Saff replied. "Apart from how warm and soft Summer's hand is." He gave it a gentle squeeze, then frowned. "Wait, I do feel something."

"If you say lust—" Huon started.

Saff held up his other hand. "Apart from that." He fixed his eyes on mine. "Do you feel that?"

"Feel what? I don't..." There, in the connection between us, a spark of magic built. It grew slowly, gradually. "I do feel that. I'm not sure if we should see what happens or step away from each other."

"You could end up covered in butterflies," Huon said.

I knew he was joking, but his expression was serious.

"Something is coming." Saff's eyes glazed. "Not butterflies," he added, so I knew he could still hear us.

"Khat, can you sense anything bad coming?" Huon asked.

"Not bad," Khat replied. "Not good either though. Just—something."

"As much as I'd love to be reassured by that, I'm

finding it hard right now," I said. "Can you be more specific?"

"You're calling it," Khat said sharply. "You tell us."

I stared at Saff. "Please tell me it's not a moth?"

"You don't like moths?" he asked.

"Of course I do, who doesn't like moths?" I asked. "But since you said it wasn't butterflies, maybe it's moths."

His mouth formed an O. "I think they only come out at night."

"He's right, they do," Fletcher said. "Plus whatever is coming is bigger than that." He stood with his hand to his forehead to shield his eyes from the sun. "Scratch that, *they* are bigger than that. And they have wings."

"They? Is there any chance whatever we're accidentally calling isn't going to kill us?" I asked.

"I'm sure it's nothing you can't blow up, love," Saff said assuringly.

"Unless it blows us up first," Khat said.

"I didn't come all this way to be killed by... anything!" Calla said.

"We'll keep you safe," Daffin said. He gestured for his team and Tavar to array themselves around us.

"They're coming closer," Fletcher said. "I can

almost make out… No way!" He dropped his hand and shook his head before he put it back up again.

"What?" I asked frantically.

"It looks like…dragons," he said. "Two of them."

"I told you dragons were real," Khat said.

"I thought they'd be bigger." Fletcher sounded disappointed.

For a moment I didn't understand. Then I realised, they weren't far away, they were just small. None was longer than my forearm.

They circled us before they came in to land on my shoulder and Saff's. Their scaled, silver bodies glittered in the sunshine.

The one who landed on me peered at me through slitted eyes, like a cat.

"You called?" The dragon's voice was deep, like that of a male Fae.

"Are you sure these are the ones?" The other dragon spoke softer. I decided she was a female.

"I'm certain, dear," the male replied. "I am Kadagan. My mate is Temara."

"Fancy names for dragons," Saff said, his eyes wide and staring.

"You're well-informed regarding dragon names?" Kadagan asked.

"Considering I didn't know you existed until two minutes ago, I'm going to say no," Saff replied.

Kadagan sniffed. A tendril of smoke slipped from his nostril. "Why did you call us then?"

"Um." I hesitated. "I'm not sure it wasn't an accident. You see we're trying to return lesser magic to—"

"Why didn't you say so?" Kadagan asked. "We've waited a long time for you." He scratched his head with one of his hind feet. "You would say it was a long time, wouldn't you, dear?"

"A very long time," Temara replied. She bobbed her head.

"If you don't mind me asking, where did you come from?" I asked.

"We live in the land beyond the ocean," Temara replied. "Which is just a fancy name for another part of the realm." She surveyed the land around us. "It's bad there, but not as bad as this."

"This seems to be the heart of the taint," I said. "We're supposed to find the answer here, apparently."

"It seems logical to assume the place where it began might hold the answers." Temara hopped down from Saff's shoulder and landed on the dirt. She tucked her wings back and began to grow larger.

As she did, her form began to change. Dragon legs became longer. Her front two became arms, her back legs like a Fae. Her face became shorter and hair replaced scales, still the same glittering silver.

In a matter of moments she stood in front of me, a silver-hair Fae with wings like mine. Beside her, Kadagan was slightly taller, but now a muscular man, his bare chest sculpted as though made from living stone.

I managed to close my mouth and stop staring. "That's why we didn't know dragons existed," I said once I regained my voice. "You're Fae with the ability to shift."

"That's correct," Temara smiled kindly.

"Why reveal yourselves now?" Huon asked.

"We too face a slow death," Temara said. "If the price of hiding is extinction, it's too high."

"That makes sense," Huon replied. "How can you help us find the last key? It's supposed to be here."

"You should watch them," Calla said. I had all but forgotten she was there. Now I remembered, I turned to her in surprise.

"I have heard of the silver Fae," Calla said. "Read about them in books. They will have their own agenda. Perhaps they caused the taint and have come to stop us."

I frowned at her. "You heard Khat, he said they aren't evil." I gestured toward the mimicat.

"He also said they aren't good," Calla reminded me.

I frowned. "Who of us can claim to be good?"

Silence fell.

Saff raised his hand. "I have my moments, but I wouldn't say I'm good, as such."

"Me either," Huon said. "I mean, I do my best, but I'm not perfect."

"I'm far from perfect," Fletcher said.

"I'm close to perfect," Khat said, "but I wouldn't claim to be good either."

I gave Calla a look and she grimaced.

"Don't say I didn't warn you," she said.

"Noted," I replied. I turned back to Temara. "Huon had a good question. How can you help?"

"The lore was handed down from generation to generation," Temara said. Her eyes glazed as she appeared to be thinking. "When the dragons are called, they must heed. Only when the heart lies in flames can the key be revealed." She blinked and shrugged.

"It looks as though there's already been some fire through here," I pointed out.

"This is not the precise heart," Kadagan said. "We

need to find the centre of the taint."

"How do we do that?" Saff asked.

"We look," Tavar said. "The ground and flora become worse as we travel north-west. If we continue that way, we may see… something."

"*Something* is very vague, troll," Calla growled.

"Her name is Tavar," I said darkly.

Calla rolled her eyes and shrugged. "My point remains. What are we looking for?"

"You were the one who read all those books," I said sharply, "you tell us."

Huon clicked his fingers. "It's a place. I mean, ruins like the ones we found in… in the forest."

I felt the blood drain from my face. "I've been there. I mean, sort of. When Rosette spoke to me on the island where we found the second key, she showed me images of her past. One of those was the place Myrta used to change Fae into trullen."

Calla flinched.

"You read about Myrta?" I asked.

"In several of the older books," she replied. "Myrta was quite the visionary, from what I know."

"She was a nutcase," I said dryly. "Why would the ancients have left a key there? Surely that's the first place Myrta would look if she got back here?"

"Maybe they assumed she would think it too

obvious," Huon said. "Although it's probably hidden under more puzzles."

"That's true." I ran a hand over my hair. "Calla, do you have any idea where this place might be?"

"I think I do, yes," she replied. "I memorised a map of the area some time ago." She looked gleeful.

I should feel the same, we were almost at the end of this journey, but after all I'd seen and done, I would save my joy for later.

I studied my sister's face. One thing which was certain, if Myrta inhabited Zinnia's mind and body, Calla was unaware of it. The mention of Myrta would have horrified her. I considered telling her, but decided against it. We might be able to trust the silver Fae and we might not. I couldn't discount the idea they'd been waiting for her all this time, not for us.

I wanted to trust them. I needed to. We needed all the allies we could get, especially if we weren't successful.

I gave my head a shake and snuck over closer to Saff. "You were right, they aren't butterflies," I whispered.

He chuckled. "No, butterflies aren't that hot." He put an arm around me and drew me close for a long, searing kiss. "You're still hotter," he said once he pulled back.

"I don't know about that," I replied. I felt plain beside Temara. The term impossibly good looking came to mind and I sighed. I pushed the thought away. None of that mattered right now.

"I do." Saff squeezed my ass cheeks and kissed me again. "I'll show you again, the next chance we get."

I laughed softly and moved over to Tavar.

Next stop, Myrta's ancient den of evil.

CHAPTER NINE

"As notorious places of evil go, this is underwhelming," Huon declared.

I had to agree. The land was a desolate plain, devoid of everything but the stumps of old trees and a few blocks of stone. I'd half expected bleached bones and the howls of tortured souls left behind the guard the location.

I poked a block with my toe and chunks crumbled away.

"It seems to be around the right age," I said, my tone as dry as the dust on my boots.

"I don't suppose there's a key lying under the stone there?" Huon asked.

"Not that I saw," I replied. "But I know for a fact it

wouldn't be that easy." I gestured toward Temara. "You said something about the heart lying in flames?"

"There's nothing here to burn," Saff said, "except my poor skin. I'll have more freckles than there are stars in the sky if we're out here much longer."

"You should wear a hat," Fletcher said.

"Thanks buddy," Saff squinted at him. "I'll remember that next time we travel to a desert."

"You're welcome, Saffo," Fletcher said ironically.

"Try being a blonde," Huon said, his hand over his face.

"I hear you," I agreed. "Now, about the fire. That could be a metaphor for something, I suppose."

"Or literally a fire," Kadagan said.

I waited for him to say more, but he moved away from us. Before I could ask, he shifted back into a dragon.

"Right, fire-breathing," Saff muttered. "I think this is where we all stand the hells back."

"That would be wise," Temara said. She gestured toward us and shifted. This time they became larger dragons, maybe twice my size, with enormous wingspans.

"Who says size doesn't matter?" Huon looked admiringly at their silver wings.

"Those who know it's not what you have but how you use it," I told him.

"Good answer." He nodded his approval. "I wish I knew what this would—woah!" He leapt back as Kadagan belched out a blast of flame.

I threw up my hand to shield my face from the heat, only to lower it when the flame hit something solid. It diverted around the sides of— What the hells was that?

"The building is still here," Huon said. "It's hidden."

"Well shit," I muttered. Of course it was.

Kadagan stopped flaming and the building disappeared again.

The smell of smoke and hot stone was thick in the air, but it dissipated in a matter of moments.

I stepped forward, hand out, and felt around where the fire had been.

"Be careful, it might be hot," Huon warned.

"I am," I said over my shoulder. "There's nothing here. At least, nothing I can feel or see." No sign of anything remained.

"Let's try with two of us," Temara said. "Step back."

I moved as quickly as I could without tripping

over my feet. Huon grabbed my arm and pulled me to his side.

Temara and Kadagan shot out twin blasts of flame. As before, the building was visible until the fire was gone.

"Calla, did any of the books say anything about this?" I asked.

"No," she said, her eyes intent on the space in front of us. She looked fascinated, but not worried.

As for me, I wished Kale was here, he might know what we were supposed to do.

"Can you dragons try again?" Huon suggested. "Maybe for a bit longer?"

Temara took a moment to confer quietly with her husband. They whispered and murmured, but finally nodded in agreement.

"We'll try again," Temara said.

One large dragon flaming was hot. Two with prolonged flame was an inferno. I felt as though all the skin on my body might sear away in the oven of heat.

I pressed my hands against my eyes. The backs of my hands became so hot they almost hurt. I staggered back. Tears poured from my eyes.

Just when it became too much, the heat was gone.

The air fell still. The smell of burning filled my nostrils.

I lowered my hands.

The structure, a long, low house, stood intact on the ground where before there was nothing. Every stone was in place as if it was laid yesterday. Even the wooden door looked solid and untouched by time.

"That's definitely a first," I muttered.

"Yes it is. Do you think it's safe?" Huon asked. He eyed the structure as though it might disappear again, but it didn't.

Temara and her husband were already back in Fae form, but made no move to step any closer to the structure.

"We will go inside first," Daffin declared.

Tavar nodded and pulled out a knife.

Calla stepped forward and for a moment I thought she might disagree.

"They should check it's safe first," I told her. "Isn't that what they're here for?"

Calla hesitated and nodded. "The ancients might have left traps for us," she agreed. "Better they trip them."

My eyebrows shot up. "That wasn't what I meant—"

She gave me a wave of dismissal and stepped in behind the trolls.

It was then I became aware of it; the key was warm and trying to push me inside the structure.

"It's in there," I whispered to Huon.

He turned to me slowly, eyes wide, and nodded. "I can feel it."

My lips parted. So Kale was right, he *was* the third foretold. I took his hand and squeezed it.

Thank the gods it wasn't Calla.

"Kale should be here," I said softly.

Huon sighed. "I know, but he's got our back," Huon said. "Someone needs to deal with Zinnia."

I knew he meant Myrta, but couldn't mention her in front of the silver Fae.

"I hope he's all right," I said.

"She won't hurt him, she knows we need him for this," Huon assured me. "She's waited this long, she'll wait another few days."

He was right, in theory, but he hadn't felt her malevolence. She was so dark, so twisted, she wouldn't care who she harmed or killed to get her way.

"We will stay out here," Temara declared. "This is a place of great darkness. The smell of despair lingers."

"I didn't know despair had a smell." Saff sniffed the air. "What do you know, it does smell kinda nasty. Is that the…what do you call it?" He waved toward Fletcher.

"Stale air?" Fletcher asked. "Full of bacteria and stuff?"

"Yeah, that," Saff agreed.

"It probably is," Fletcher agreed. "It'll be worse when we open the door."

"Time to step back then," Saff said, and did so.

Daffin nodded to one of his team. She placed a hand on the door handle and twisted. It clicked audibly and swung inward.

A whoosh sounded, followed by a rush of particles which glittered in the sunlight. The moment they came into contact with the troll, she disintegrated.

One minute she was there, the next she was gone. Nothing remained but motes which sparkled before they landed on the ground at our feet.

"Dear gods," I breathed.

"Everyone move back," Huon ordered. "Back, out of range of—whatever that was."

"How far is its range?" Fletcher asked. Clearly the question was rhetorical. No one even knew what happened, much less what kind of reach it had.

We retreated about twenty metres and watched the building carefully. It didn't collapse or shake. Yet. Whatever happened to the poor troll, it didn't seem to be chasing us.

"You were right," Saff told Fletcher. "Old air is deadly."

"Yeah… that wasn't what I meant though," Fletcher said slowly. "It usually makes people sick and then they slowly die. That's where the myth of the mummy's curse came from."

"The what?" Saff looked confused.

"Uh, never mind, I'll explain later. Are we sure she's dead?" Fletcher asked.

"Unless that was another portal," Huon replied, "then I don't know what else that was."

I stepped closer to Tavar. "Have you ever seen anything like this?" I asked as gently as I could.

She regarded me with a blank expression. "That isn't how trolls usually die, no. It didn't look like a portal either."

"It was a magic trap," Calla declared.

"Don't tell me, you read that in a book too?" I regarded her through narrowed eyes. If she'd known this was coming, but hadn't said anything…

"It's obvious, isn't it?" she asked with a sniff. "What else would it be? And in answer to your question, yes, I read about magic traps. I *did* say to keep a lookout for them."

"Yes, you did." Huon nodded. "What else should we expect to encounter?"

Calla wrung her hands. "I can't be certain. Time has undoubtedly eroded the magic to the point where it may behave in unexpected ways."

"Oh really?" I grimaced. "What in the gods' names was that *supposed* to do then?"

"Possibly a warning," Calla said vaguely. "And maybe it was supposed kill intruders."

I shuddered. "Is there any chance it will go off again if anyone else tries to go inside?" That was also a rhetorical question.

"Why would the ancients set a trap?" Saff asked. "I mean, if they intended us to go inside, why not just let us inside?"

"Maybe they didn't know about the trap," I reasoned. "I suppose it's possible it only kills trolls." I looked to where Daffin stood with his team, pale-faced and anxious. None of this was his fault, but he wouldn't see it that way. The troll was a member of his team. He would feel responsible. I wished I knew what to say to make him feel better, but my brain was a blank.

"She died doing her duty," Tavar said. "The gods

will know this and see her cared for."

If that was supposed to comfort me, it didn't. A woman died. The first of many if we failed. The last if I had anything to say about it.

I nodded. Without thinking, I started forward, toward the structure.

"Summer, what the fuck?" Huon blurted out.

"Someone has to go in next," I said over my shoulder. "It can't be a troll. You heard what Calla said."

"That was a guess." He trotted to catch up with me and grabbed my hand. He swung me around to face him. "You're not risking yourself."

"Whoever tries will be at risk," I replied simply. "The realm needs you; Fletcher is human and might be at the same risk as the trolls. Saff and I have some kind of bond. He'll know if I get transported somewhere else." There was Calla, but I doubted she would willingly try.

Huon frowned. "I'm pretty sure we've had this conversation before about how *I* need you." His eyes insisted I listen, to understand and not do anything rash. For a moment, I almost considered giving in.

In the end, I couldn't.

"I think so," I agreed. "You didn't talk me out of it

then, you won't now. Don't make me blast you out of the way," I added jokingly.

He smiled wryly. "As if you would." He leaned in to claim my mouth in a rough kiss.

I kissed him back and slid my tongue over his lips before I pulled back. "I should do this before I change my mind."

"Or I could keep kissing you until you do," he said.

"Not gonna happen," I told him. I kissed his cheek and started back toward the building. My heart pounded. I was only too aware I could be wrong about this. Had the troll felt any pain before she died?

I suspected not, it was all over so quickly. She might not have even been aware of it.

I stepped carefully, eyes and nostrils open for signs of traps and toxic air.

Something crunched under my boots. I grimaced. I didn't want to think too much about what—or who —I had trodden on.

I took a shallow breath and crossed the threshold.

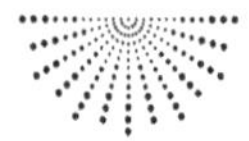

CHAPTER TEN

"I'm not dead," I called over my shoulder. Under my breath I added, "Yet."

"That's good," Huon replied. "Neither am I." He was right behind me. He must have crept up when I was focused on entering.

"You clearly don't understand the concept of me going first to make sure you're safe," I said dryly.

"Oh, I understand," he said. "I decided not to allow you to go inside alone."

"Have I told you lately you're a brat?" I asked.

He rubbed his chin. "Not lately, no. It's been at least a few days."

"I'm clearly slipping," I said. "I'll be sure to work on that."

He chuckled.

"I can remind you," Saff said from behind Huon. Fletcher peered over his shoulder.

"None of you are supposed to be here," I growled. "Can't any of you listen?"

"We can," Saff replied easily. "I just decided if you're in this, so am I."

"Me too," Fletcher said. "We're a team, the four of us, and Kale."

"Don't ask me why I'm here." Khat wound through our legs. "Put it down to a momentary lapse in sanity."

"That sounds accurate," Saff said. "Although, I thought you wanted to save the realms too?"

"I do, but I should let you Fae take the risks. I could have a nap instead." He dropped to the floor at my feet and licked his paw.

"You know what I think?" I said. "I think you're actually noble and don't want to admit it. You hide it behind a facade of snark."

"My snark is not a facade," he retorted. "It's one hundred percent genuine."

I snorted. "Fair enough." There was no arguing with him, I supposed. "We should look around."

I glanced at the guys in the hope they'd stay put in the entryway, but none would give a centimetre.

"Can I at least ask you to stay behind me?" I asked, hopeful.

"You can ask, but we're all in this," Huon replied. "This is a strange, fucking place."

I sighed and turned back to look at our surroundings. Like the tower on the island, it was made from large stones, each neatly cut. Where those stones were black, these were white. Each one looked like new.

"There's still glass in the windows," Fletcher marvelled. "It's a little dirty, but…" He raised a hand toward a pane.

"Maybe we shouldn't touch anything." I peered through the grimy windows. Tavar and the other trolls stood near the silver Fae. They all looked anxious, although Tavar appeared the calmest of them. I knew her well enough to know the way her mouth drew up at the side signalled worry, but she otherwise seemed serene.

"Can you feel the key now?" I asked Huon. Mine continued to push me forward, but the direction was vague at best. The closest I could interpret was, 'Up ahead.'

Considering the length of the building and the fact more magic likely concealed something, potentially more nasty surprises, that wasn't especially helpful.

"Just the general direction," Huon replied. He waved in front of us, confirming he had no more information than I did.

I moved out of the narrow entryway and into a bigger room lined with windows and doors. All of the doors, each plain wood, were closed.

"Don't tell me," Fletcher said. "If we pick the right door, we can go through. If we choose the wrong one, we die."

"Is that a thing you humans do?" Saff seemed genuinely curious.

"Only in movies," Fletcher replied. "If this was a movie, we'd have to solve a riddle which would tell us which door is the right one."

"That sounds like something the ancients would do," Huon agreed. "But if this was Myrta's home, we can't be sure of anything."

"We can be sure there are more traps," Calla said as she walked through the front door behind us.

I scowled at her, but she ignored me.

"What kind of traps?" Huon asked.

A frown crossed her forehead. "I'm not certain what might remain. The ancients could have dismantled them. Or put in some of their own."

Her turn of phrase made me stare at her for a moment. A thought formed in the back of my mind, but I dismissed it. She'd spent the last five years reading, it was only natural to expect her to forget some of it.

"What about Fletcher's theory about riddles?" I asked. "Should we look for those? What would they even look like?"

"It can't hurt to keep an eye out for those," she agreed. "They could be anywhere and appear to be anything." She stayed close to the doorway and cast wary eyes around the room.

"What have we seen already?" Huon mused. "The anchor, the symbol on the trapdoor."

"My blood dripping on the ground," I said dryly.

"Right." He nodded. "I don't see an anchor or the symbol. We could try my blood." He pulled out a knife and pierced his finger with the tip of the blade. A bead of blood welled. He put the knife away and squeezed until blood dripped from his finger and onto the floor.

We waited.

And waited.

"I guess it's not blood this time," I said finally.

Huon wiped his hand on his shirt and looked disappointed. "That would have made things simple."

"Too simple maybe," I said. "Nothing has been that easy yet."

"That's true," he agreed. "I suppose we need to choose a door and open it."

"If a human is safe in here, perhaps the trolls would be," Calla said. "We could have them come in and open one." She sounded as if she relished the idea.

"I'm not going to let them try," I said firmly. "We've already lost one of them."

"Better them than—" Calla caught my look and met it with one of her own. After at least a minute, she looked away. "Fine, but don't say I didn't warn you."

"Noted," I said darkly. "But check your racism at the door. I'm done hearing it." I stomped away toward a door.

Nothing about this door suggested it was any different to the others. It was the same height and width and was as plain as the rest. Funny, I would have expected Myrta to have had ostentatiously decorated doors. Maybe with screaming, tortured beings carved into the surface. Or plans for the end of the worlds and the births of ones in which she was some kind of goddess.

I pressed my palm to the wood. It felt cool under

my skin, but it didn't explode or suck me into some new plane of existence. I also felt no sense of the key being on the other side. If there was anything dangerous, it wasn't worth opening the door and letting it loose.

On the other hand, my curiosity got the better of me. This was Myrta's home. Anything we found here might help us defeat her later.

I twisted the knob and opened the door slowly. It creaked from centuries of disuse, the first sign of the building's true age.

I shoved it harder and jumped back a few steps.

"Summer, are you all right?" Huon sounded frantic.

"I'm fine," I replied. "Just getting out of the way of the stale air."

"Oh." Relief flooded his face. "Well—good. Is there anything in there?"

I didn't see any glittering particles or blasts of magic aimed at my head, so I stepped back to the doorway and peered inside.

"It's..." I swivelled my head to look carefully around the dark room. "It's empty." My boots kicked up dust on the tiled floor as I walked inside, but that was all. There was no furniture or any sign any had ever been there.

I crouched and blew the dust off a section of floor. Dark brown stains dotted the tiles here and there. It didn't take a genius to guess what they were.

Khat meandered over and sniffed at them. "Blood," he declared.

"I guessed," I told him.

"Fae blood," he added.

"Oh." I should have figured that part out myself. "Of course it is." I cocked my head. "You can tell that from the smell of thousand year old blood?"

"Fae blood is Fae blood," he replied. "Humans and trolls smell different."

"It could be from a trullen," I pointed out. "Back then, they weren't so far removed from Fae."

"True, but it's Fae," he said firmly.

I waited for him to add more, but he slunk back out of the room.

"All right then," I muttered to myself. I stood and followed him. "One down, five to go."

Huon nodded. "It would be easier if one of them had a sign. 'The key is behind this door,' or something like that."

I snorted softly. "That brings us back to what I said before about none of this being easy."

He sighed dramatically. "I suppose it's my turn to pick a door."

"Who says we're taking turns?" I shot back.

"I do," he said. "I'm still king, aren't I?"

"First of all," I counted the points off on my fingers, "no, you're not, according to Zinnia. Second, if I marry you, I'll be queen. That means I'll really be in charge." I gave him a look of pure innocence.

He returned it with a slow smile and shake of his head. "No. No, you won't."

I drew myself up taller, as if I stood a chance of looking imposing. "Will too," I said and raised my chin.

"Not a chance." He tilted his head and raised a brow. "We'll be equals."

I feigned a scowl. "Fine, equals. But you'll still do what I say"

He threw back his head and laughed.

I broke into a grin. We were both strong-willed and knew the other would only do what we said if they wanted to.

"I'll do whatever you say," Saff said helpfully. "Especially if it involves harder, deeper, more…" He batted his eyelashes at me.

"It undoubtedly will," I replied. "But we should be looking for the key."

"Right." Saff nodded. "The key." He scrutinised

each door in turn. "I've come to the conclusion that I have no conclusion. They're all the bloody same."

"They are, aren't they?" Fletcher sounded frustrated. Without warning, he marched toward a door and swung it open. He covered his mouth and nose with his sleeve and waited.

"It's a bedroom," he said finally. "Or it was once."

Unlike the rest of the building, this room looked as though it had suffered all the effects of time. What was once a quilt had decayed to the point where it might fall apart if anyone touched it. A bed frame and side table looked equally delicate. The whole room smelled musty and rotten.

"Dust," Fletcher said slowly, his brow creased.

"There's dust everywhere," I agreed.

"No, I mean, it had to get in somehow," he said. "The magic which hid it hasn't kept it in a total bubble."

"I suppose so," I agreed. "Magic isn't perfect."

He gave a short, bitter laugh. "That's too fucking true." His expression darkened. "If air got in, other things might have."

I flinched. "Like bugs and things?"

"It's possible." He poked the bed frame with his toe. The section he touched crumbled and fell to the floor. Dust rose and spun before it settled back down.

"There's nothing useful here," Huon declared. "We need to try another door."

I nodded and followed him back out. The moment I stepped past the threshold a chill travelled down my spine.

I froze. The hairs on my arms rose.

"What?" Fletcher asked.

"I don't know. I feel as if…"

"…we just awakened something." Huon finished.

"Something big," I added.

"Very big," he agreed. "Enormous. Hungry."

"I was already awake," Saff quipped.

I shook my head at him. I would have laughed, but this was…oppressive. It was harder to breathe. It pressed down on my mind. Thoughts moved slowly, like honey on a winter's day.

The door at the end of the room flew open and slammed against the wall.

I jumped.

"Oh gods."

CHAPTER ELEVEN

"Tiny?" The huge dog bounded up to me and put his paws on my chest. "How in the seven hells did you get here?"

He panted at me, doggy breath hot on my face. His tail wagged so fast it was a blur.

"Oh, right, you can't talk." I patted his head. "Is Jude with you?"

"Rick?" Fletcher shouted and headed off toward the doorway at a run.

"Wait!" Huon called after him. "It might still be a trap."

Fletcher slowed to a walk, but didn't stop. "Rick?" he called out again.

I exchanged glances with Huon. "I guess we should follow."

He nodded his agreement.

Gently, I pushed Tiny off me. His tail kept wagging and his tongue lolled out the side of his mouth.

"Come on, boy," I said, "let's see if Jude is here too." Maybe then someone would explain the fuck was going on.

"Are you sure that's really Tiny?" Saff asked. He eyed the dog doubtfully.

Tiny trotted over to a doorframe, cocked a leg and peed.

"Sure seems like him to me," I said dryly. I shook my head but smiled. No matter what happened, Tiny was always just Tiny. Well—huge, but himself.

"It's him all right," Khat said. "Stink and all."

"What in the name of the gods is it?" Calla asked. Her eyes were huge.

"He's a dog," I replied. "Last seen stranded on an island in the human realm, with his owner, Jude, and Fletcher's brother."

"And a Seafae," Saff added.

"Yes, and Yina the Seafae." What were the chances of her being here as well? We were a damned long way from any water.

I peered into the room and my breath caught again.

"So this was what I felt before," I said softly.

In the centre of the room were three columns of magic. Each one stretched from floor to ceiling. A person was suspended in each. Their arms stuck out to their sides as if they floated in water.

"Rick," Fletcher whispered. Jude was suspended beside Rick, Yina on the far end.

"I see you found them." Tavar's voice behind me startled me into twirling around.

"Oh, you got in safely," I said. "It looks like the portal sucked them in too."

"The portal, in a manner of speaking," Tavar agreed. "They had a bit of help."

I frowned at her. "I suppose so. The ancients did like to add in their tricks." No, there was something more to this.

Khat hissed at Tavar, his back arched.

"Khat, I thought we were past this," I said wearily. "Trolls are just as—"

"That's no troll," Khat said. His tail whipped. "How did you hide it?"

"Magic," Tavar replied.

I shook my head. "I don't understand."

"Of course you don't, foolish Fae," Tavar said derisively.

I stepped back. "Myrta?"

"Of course it's Myrta," Khat said. "She masked herself this time." He looked confused and furious.

"Did I?" Tavar asked.

"That or… you've been jumping from one Fae to another," I reasoned.

She inclined her head.

"Zinnia?" I guessed.

"Briefly," she agreed. "Long enough to come here and set this up."

"You bitch!" Fletcher lunged at her, but Huon and Saff grabbed him and held him back by his arms. "Let my brother go!"

"Oh I will," Tavar-Myrta smiled. "I'll even return this hideous troll to you alive. But there's a few things I need you to do first."

"We're not doing anything you say," Fletcher growled.

I held up a hand for him to calm for a moment, even though I understood his fury. Rick's life literally hung in the balance, held in the hands of an ancient evil.

"What do you want?" I asked.

"I want you to retrieve the last key," she said. "I can show you where it is, but I can't get it. It resists the meagre abilities of this body."

"We intended to do that anyway," Huon said coldly.

"I don't understand what's going on," Calla said. "Did you say this was… Myrta? *The* Myrta?"

"Oh, you've heard of me," Myrta said. She looked Calla up and down. "How nice. I did think about taking your body, but you were actually guiding them here. I thought you would come under suspicion much sooner than the troll would."

"I suspected she was Myrta," Khat grumbled.

"I…" Calla paled. "I've never… I don't…"

I patted her arm. "It's all right, we know. You were fangirling over her."

"Your sisters are Fae after my own heart," Myrta told me. "One wants power over her own people. The other—" She nodded toward Calla. "She thinks much further ahead. Don't you, Calla?"

"I… I…" Calla stammered. "I don't know what you mean."

"Of course you do," Myrta said shortly. "You crave the dark magic. You want what I want—to return dark magic to all the realms. To hold the ultimate power of life and death over those who look down on you. To create and to destroy."

"I just want Zinnia to respect me," Calla replied,

speaking toward her chest. "And Summer." She lifted her head and shot me a look of pure loathing. "I know what you thought of me."

"I didn't—" I started.

"That's right, you didn't," she hissed. "You never thought about anyone but yourself. Even this—this journey, is about making you feel good about saving everyone. If you didn't think they would adore you for it, you wouldn't bother."

I gave her a sideways look. "I see you really believe that. You obviously don't know me at all."

"I know you better than you think," Calla hissed. She turned to Myrta with a look of reverence. "We will get the keys. One is back at the capital with Kale."

A look of annoyance crossed Myrta's face. "I'm aware of that. Zinnia thinks to mate with him. I was unable to prevent him from staying behind. No matter, we will bring him to us."

"Lady Myrta." Calla licked her lips. "I freely offer you the use of my unworthy body." She held out her hands.

"Now I know you've gone crazy," I muttered. Frankly, I felt nauseous. Calla was right about one thing, I never made time for her. I couldn't recall an occasion when she'd made time for me either, but I could have tried. Regret wouldn't help me now though.

"Calla, this woman is evil," I said. "You don't want her in your head. Trust me on this."

Calla rounded on me. "Trust you? Not for any reason. Myrta was a genius. *Is* a genius. You have no idea—"

"Oh, you'd be surprised," I said. "Move out of the way, it's time to get rid of this nutcase." I raised my hands.

Myrta smiled. "If you use magic in here, it will kill me," she said, "but it will take the rest of you with me."

"You don't have magic of your own," I pointed out. "You're a parasite."

"I set up safeguards." She looked smug. "My magic remains here for me to access. Enough to see this to the end and then for a hundred years after that. It's nothing to what I will have. When I'm restored, I will have more magic than you could ever dream of." She seemed very certain of that. "Find the keys and bring them to me and I will allow you to serve me."

I snorted. "No thanks."

"You speak as though you have a choice." She

smiled again and this time the look gave me the shivers.

She turned her attention to Calla. "Thank you, child," she said. "I control this body well enough. As much as it degrades me to inhabit a troll, you're already my faithful servant. You will be my eyes and ears to ensure these Fae don't try to double cross me. If they do—" Her gaze flicked to me. "I will kill their friends, one by one."

Fletcher made a choking sound. "We might help if you let my brother go now."

Myrta laughed. "That would defeat the purpose entirely. You will do as I say or he will die. Don't worry," she added sweetly, "I'll be sure to leave him until last. As long as you cooperate. It's up to you, really."

"You're a fucked up bitch," I told her.

"She really is, isn't she?" Saff said.

"Now, now," she scolded. "Calling me names will get you nowhere. You need to look for the last key."

"I think maybe Zinnia was right," I said slowly. "We should look for a portal. Get the Fae out of the realm. It's not safe here." I looked Myrta in the eyes.

"You think to call my bluff?" She clicked her fingers and the shaft of magic which held Yina flared.

She screamed silently. Her arms flailed. Her hands curled into claws as though she might scratch her way out.

Then she burst into flames. The smell of burning flesh seared my nostrils.

She screamed again, but this time it echoed through the room, a sound of pure agony and terror.

A moment later the flames were gone and a pile of black ash fell to the floor.

Jude and Rick thrashed a little. Their mouths twisted with anguish. Their eyes were still closed, but I knew they understood what happened. The magic column around each grew wider, looked stronger. To keep three held there like that must have stretched the magic.

Fletcher let out a cry and sagged against Huon, who grunted with the effort of keeping him on his feet.

"Dear gods," I breathed. Yina hadn't stood a chance. My stomach turned. I might be sick. Maybe I could aim for Calla's shoes. "You're a monster."

"Perhaps you'd care to take her place," Myrta said to me. "To help ensure the cooperation of your lovers."

"Don't you dare," Huon growled. "We'll find the key. Just tell us where to look and we'll get it."

"Huon..." I knew that look in his eyes. He wouldn't change his mind, no matter what I said or did. I hated that our love made us so vulnerable, and that she'd so easily use it against us.

"We need to save the realm," he said firmly. "Whatever that entails." And then we would find a way to defeat Myrta.

Gods, I hope he knew what he was doing. I certainly didn't.

"Fine, where is it?" I demanded.

"Behind the middle door," Myrta replied.

I rolled my eyes. "There is no middle door. There are six of them."

"Are there?" she asked.

I looked at her sideways, then let my gaze slip to Huon.

He shrugged. "We can look." He pushed Fletcher over gently so his weight rested on Saff.

"Hey," Saff protested. "You're heavy."

Fletcher shook his head as if to clear it, then stood on his own. "Sorry. I'm fine, let's just find this bloody key and get my brother out of there."

"And Jude," Saff said. "Poor guy really did get dragged into things, didn't he?"

"He did," I agreed.

Tiny trudged over toward his human and lay down at his feet. He put his head on his paws and proceeded to drool on the floor.

"Are we really doing this?" Khat asked. He followed me toward the doorway.

"We don't have a choice," Huon said. "Don't worry, we've got this. Somehow."

"I wish I had your confidence," Khat said.

"Me too," I agreed. I stepped through the doorway and turned.

As soon as Calla followed us out, the door disappeared.

It left only smooth wall, with no hint a door was ever there.

"No!" Fletcher threw himself forward and hit his fists on the stones.

"Fletcher, it's just magic." I reached for one of his arms and Huon grabbed the other. Fletcher's hands were already red with welts and scrapes.

"Just magic?" he ground out. "My brother is behind that." A tear trickled down his cheek.

"I know," I said softly. "He's still there. When we find the key, Myrta will open it up again."

I hoped.

He hesitated, then nodded, shoulders slumped.

"On the upside," Saff said, "there's now only five doors left."

"Right." Reluctantly, I let go of Fletcher's arm, moved to stand in front of the middle door.

I turned the knob.

CHAPTER TWELVE

"This will definitely not be easy," Saff said.

I nodded my agreement. We spent the better part of the last ten minutes staring at the key. It rotated slowly, suspended in a column of magic like Jude and Rick.

"Someone is going to have to try to grab it," Huon said.

"I vote for Calla," Khat said.

"Huon is the one the key is calling to, is he not?" Calla asked.

Silence fell before Huon said, "Yes, it is."

"I still think Calla should do it," Khat said. "What's the worst that could happen?"

"Nothing," I replied.

"Exactly. At best she would be incinerated." He

licked his paw. "On second thought, maybe Myrta should try again."

"Since neither of those things is going to happen," I said, "perhaps we could discuss realistic scenarios."

"Me," Huon said. "I'm the only realistic scenario. If the key wants me, then I'll be the only one who can retrieve it."

"Or you could die," Fletcher said in a small voice.

Tiny panted and drooled on the floor near Huon's feet. I wasn't sure if that meant he agreed or not.

"I have an idea," Saff said suddenly.

"You're not trying—" Huon frowned at him.

"Not specifically," Saff agreed, "but so far we've had to do a lot by holding hands and combining our magic."

"Combining magic," I echoed.

"Summer? Are you all right?" Huon cupped my cheek with his hand and peered into my eyes.

"Hmmm? Oh, yes," I said quickly. "I was just remembering something Birch said. In order to bring back lesser magic, we would have to combine ours."

"We've done that several times now," Huon agreed.

"Right, so why not now?"

"Because you might both die," Fletcher said. He took my hand and stepped closer to me as Huon moved back. "I don't want to lose you. You're my family." He licked his lips anxiously. "I love you."

"I love you too." I kissed his mouth.

He kissed me back, hard and urgent, a silent plea not to endanger myself again.

I pulled back and sighed. "We have to try this. Huon and I."

"And me," Saff said. "I think I'm needed for this too." A frown crossed his brow and he shrugged. "I don't know how I know, I just feel it."

"Your senses have been good," I agreed.

"I'm helping as well," Fletcher said firmly. "Whatever happens to you, happens to me as well."

I wanted to refuse, but I'd never seen him look so determined. I nodded. "Fine, but you're on the end of the line so you can jump back if you need to." *If you're able too.*

"Deal," he said. "Should Kale be here for this?"

I thought for a moment. "Possibly. Maybe one of us should go back for him." I eyed Calla meaningfully.

She raised her chin. "I'm not leaving."

"It was worth a try," I said. "I suppose we'll have to

try without him. If it doesn't work, we'll have to go and get him."

"Unless you're all dead," Khat remarked.

"Yes, thank you for the reminder," I said sarcastically.

"You're welcome," he said. "I think I'll wait outside."

"That might be best," I agreed. "Calla, you should do the same. For your own safety," I added quickly. She might be out of her tree, but she was still my sister.

Although, I was starting to understand that family meant more than being related by blood. Fletcher was right; he, Saff, Huon and Kale were more family than Zinnia and Calla.

"If I die, tell our mother and father I love them," I said.

Calla blinked and for a moment I thought I saw a tear glint in her eyes. "I will. They would be sad you didn't go to see them when you were home."

"I know." I looked down at my feet for a moment. "I was busy." Excuses were too easy to make. When this was over, I would find time. I gave myself a mental shake. My list of things to do when this was over was getting longer by the day. I should start writing them all down.

"You're always busy." Calla's tone made me look back up. Her face was dark, eyes cold.

I opened my mouth to apologise, but the words wouldn't come. The gods knew I wasn't perfect, but at least I hadn't turned to an ancient, evil psychopath for validation.

I turned away from her. "We should do this."

Huon responded with a short nod and reached out for my hand. I took it and grabbed Saff's. He in turn took Fletcher's.

"This is cozy," Saff said. "If I die now, I regret not having another glass of wine at dinner last night."

I laughed softly. "I regret not bringing a jar of hazelnut chocolate spread back from the human realm with me."

"I regret being a dick to Summer for so long that she hated me when we could have been in love instead," Huon said, his eyes full of emotion.

"I regret not being nicer to you too," I replied.

"I regret not having a beer right now," Fletcher said. "This might be easier if I was drunk."

I chuckled. "Good point. All right, let's get on with this, shall we?"

Huon nodded. "I love you, Summer."

"I love you too," I said back.

"I love you as well." Saff squeezed my hand.

"I love you also," I replied.

"Yes, yes, get on with it," Calla snapped. "Myrta won't wait forever."

I swallowed. "If I die, tell Myrta she's a raging bitch."

Calla gaped, but my attention went to Huon.

He reached his hand toward the column of magic. His fingers trembled and glowed.

His fingertips disappeared inside the magic. For a moment, time stood still.

Then with an almighty tug, we were all pulled toward the column. I tried to let go of Saff's hand, but we seemed to be fused together.

"Let go of Fletcher!" I called desperately. At least one of us should make it out.

"I can't!" Saff called back.

I was sucked into a whirlwind of glowing light.

I'm so tired of being spun around, I thought.

A moment later I was thrown out again. I landed on my side with a thud, the guys' hands still in mine.

I thought we were transported to somewhere different, yet again, but we lay on the floor in the same room. The magic column remained. The key still rotated inside it.

"Is everyone all right?" Huon asked.

I muttered my agreement and the others nodded.

"Well, that was a bust," Saff said.

"I guess we need Kale." I let go of the guy's hands and rubbed my ass.

"Or souls," Huon said. "They've guarded every key but this one."

"Right." I nodded slowly. "There doesn't seem to be any here though."

"Except Yina's," Fletcher said softly.

"Yes, except hers." I sighed sadly. "And that first troll." Gods, I didn't even know her name.

"If souls are needed, I could ask Myrta to kill the other two," Calla said as if she was discussing the weather.

"No!" Fletcher climbed to his feet and stalked toward her.

She retreated to the doorway. "Do you have a better solution, human?"

"Myrta is a soul," he retorted. "She could offer herself as sacrifice."

"No, she will not be doing that." Myrta stepped into the room. Her sudden appearance made Calla jump. "This building is protected by magic which keeps out such incursions."

"Except by you," I pointed out.

"I was in a body at the time," she replied. "If the key requires the sacrifice of souls, I can arrange that."

"We also need Kale," I said. "In fact, we probably just need him." I had no idea if that was the case, but I wanted him here, with me. With us.

"He already comes," she said with a superior smile. "I left word with Zinnia to ready the Fae. She will have been told by now. And where to come."

Calla looked furious. "My sister may not bend to your will," she said awkwardly. I saw on her face her reluctance to let Zinnia near Myrta. She didn't want our sister chosen above her. Gods, her insecurity would kill us all.

"She will bend," Myrta said, "or she will die."

That seemed to satisfy Calla, but she still looked somewhat uneasy.

"It looks like we'll have to wait then." I leaned back against the wall and crossed my arms. Tiny trotted over and lay down beside me, his head on my leg.

Calla scowled as if annoyed that yet another male favoured me.

I returned her look and patted Tiny on the head.

She looked away.

I closed my eyes and rested my head on the wall behind me. Without a word, I reached my senses out, probed for—I don't know what, maybe some hint of Yina's soul, or those set to guard the final key. I felt something, but it slipped away before I could get a good grasp of whatever it was. I had a hint of longing and suffering, but patience as well.

I licked my lips and tried again. This time it came to me.

We need to be free, a voice said, soft and lyrical, as though it sang rather than spoke.

Where are you? I thought back. I couldn't rule out the idea they only existed in my imagination.

I heard a tinkling laugh, which dispelled that idea.

We are real. We are tied to this place. Do you not see us?

I opened my eyes a crack. *No, I can't see you, I can only hear you.*

Can you feel us? Something soft touched the side of my neck. It slipped downward, inside my shirt, to the top of my breast.

Um, I feel that. Who are you? What are you?

We are—us, the voices, I couldn't make out how many, sounded confused. *We were made to serve. To please the Fae. Do we please you?*

They sounded so hopeful I swallowed and said, *Of course you do. Are you here to help? Can you let us get to the key? It's stuck into the magic. We need to get it out so we can keep the realm alive.* Should I expect sympathy from beings long since dead?

My heart sank when they replied with, *We cannot touch the key. The magic has locked us out. Kept us from our duty. The magic needs to be lowered. We can touch you though. We can please you.*

What do you mean? I asked.

Warm, ghostly fingers slid around my breast, almost making me gasp out loud. I bit my lip.

You probably shouldn't do that, I said. My pulse raced.

The fingers withdrew. *You are displeased.* The voices sounded as if they might cry.

No, I replied. *No, I'm just surrounded by Fae, humans and trolls who might not understand.*

They cannot see us, the voices said.

They can see me, I replied. The gods knew I was curious as to what these voices were and what they could do, but not like this. Not in front of Myrta and Calla. And not without the guys' knowledge. They didn't mind sharing me with each other, but I wouldn't cheat, especially with random voices which might only exist in my head.

Do you know how to bring the magic down? I asked.

You must do it, the voices answered.

How?

Would it please you if we showed you how?

It would please me very much, I assured them.

We must take you to a place, they said. *You will see through the eyes of another. Then you will know. Your body will stay here. The others will not know. She must not know. If she knows, she will stop us.*

I assumed they meant Myrta. *All right, do whatever you need to do.*

I held my breath and waited.

CHAPTER THIRTEEN

"What do you want?" I asked. Only, it wasn't me. I tried to glance down at the body I was in, but I couldn't move. For a moment I started to panic, thinking Myrta had taken control of me again. Then I realised— This was just a memory. This was how things happened. I couldn't change it, I could only sit back and watch.

A man sat opposite me. A Fae. I saw the curve of his wings behind muscular shoulders. His body was sculpted like it was chiselled out of marble. I would have stared if this was my own body. This body stared too.

He smiled. "I want to watch you pleasure yourself."

I frowned. What did this have to do with magic?

Gods, these souls seemed to be a horny bunch.

Even though this was a memory, I felt her desire. My body was on fire for this man.

"I'm supposed to bear a child," I said.

He smiled slowly and moved toward me. "Oh, you will." He slipped his hands under my shirt and palmed my nipples. "I will fuck you until you get pregnant. But first, I want to see you pleasure yourself." He dropped his hands and undid my trousers. He pulled them down and tossed them aside.

"Take off the rest of your clothes," he said. "Strip for me." He sat back on the bed and crossed his arms.

I stood and slowly unbuttoned my shirt. I let it slide off my arms. My eyes on his, I unhooked my bra and took it off, one side, then the other. I turned my back and slipped my panties down to my ankles.

I caught a glimpse of the window and the view outside. The garden was green and lush. I knew what this place was. This was Myrta's lair, the place she conducted experiments. The place she created the trullen from unborn Fae.

This pair was a part of that. A willing pair to be sure, but still…

I lay back on the bed and parted my legs in such a way he could see everything. His cock hardened and pushed at the front of his pants.

I ran a hand over my breast, palmed my nipple and groaned at the sensation which washed over me.

"I want you," I told him.

"I know." He gave a sly smile, but didn't move.

I slipped my hand down between my legs and found my clit. With the tips of two fingers, I rubbed at it, lightly at first.

He undid his trousers and opened them to take his cock in his hand. He rubbed his hand up and down his length.

I moaned at the sight and rubbed harder. "I need you." I panted.

"I want you to come," he said. "Then you get my cock."

I focused my eyes on him and rubbed faster. The pressure in my body built until it was almost unbearable.

He licked his lips.

I imagined his tongue licking me.

My mouth went dry. Desire rose faster than lighting. It washed over me, hard and fast. I rocked against my fingers and let out a cry of pleasure.

Quicker than I'd have thought possible, he was up over me. He pulled my hand away and pressed my fingers into his mouth.

"Mmm." He sucked on them for a moment, then

pushed his rock hard cock inside me. He lay still for a while, then proceeded to pound into me, frantic and hot.

"Gods, yes," he breathed. He stopped, his breath coming out his nose in gasps. He rolled me over and pinned me beneath him. His cock slid back into me. "You please me. You will please me more when you bear my child."

I murmured something which sounded as though I was happy to please him.

He fucked me so hard it almost hurt, but it felt so good. He leaned in and bit my shoulder.

My eyes watered, but I said nothing.

Again he pulled out and rolled me onto my back. He pushed my legs up over his shoulders and slammed into my pussy, all the way to his balls. With a grunt, he drew back and slammed in again.

I cried out in pain this time, but he only smiled and did it again and again.

Tears slid down my cheeks. He licked one away, then grunted. His thrusts became quick, frantic. I knew he was on the edge.

He dropped over the edge with a low cry and pumped into my body with deliberate strokes, milking himself for every drop of cum he could.

Finally he sagged and I lowered my legs. He lay on top of me, heavy and trying to catch his breath.

"Of all the jobs I have," he said eventually, "this is by far my favourite."

I laughed softly, but it lacked sincerity. "Mine too." My body would ache from the rough fucking he gave me, but I was doing my duty by Lady Myrta. "Do you think it worked this time?"

"If not, I'll fuck you again." He pulled out of me and rolled onto his back. "And again, until it does."

I felt pleased at this. Apparently whoever's body I was in, she was more interested in his attention than doing her so-called duty. He was handsome enough, but he didn't seem especially fond of this woman he'd just fucked.

"I will be willing to do that," I replied.

A sneer crossed his features, but it was gone almost immediately and replaced by a smug smile.

"Of course you will. You've been nothing but willing."

For some reason, his words filled me with shame, as though having desire was a bad thing. If I could, I would have told him to fuck off. Whoever she was, she deserved better. Then again, she *was* working with Myrta.

I sighed to myself. *What does this have to do with*

magic?

The man slapped my ass and got up to dress. "I'll see you later." He gave her half a glance and hurried away.

I sighed. I waited until he left and got up. With water from a jug on the table, I gave myself a thorough clean, especially my pussy. Evidently pregnancy wasn't as high on her list of priorities as she'd let on.

I dressed and moved to the door. I pressed my ear against it and listened. I heard no sound from outside.

Gingerly, I turned the knob and eased it open. No one stood in the corridor outside.

I crept a few steps, then straightened up and walked to the kitchen. Nothing looked more suspicious than skulking around. Evidently I was allowed to be here, but I was up to something.

I could do with a snack, but what does this have to do with magic? Of course there was no answer from either the souls or the woman whose body I was in.

Myrta stood near the window. She spoke in a low voice to the man who had fucked me. He gave her a slow smile and a nod. She scowled and stalked toward the doorway. She stopped when she saw me and her eyes narrowed.

I curtsied.

She sniffed and walked past me and out the door. She was so close I could have reached out and stran-gled her. I wanted to, both me and the woman who owned this body. I couldn't, and she didn't dare.

The door closed behind her.

"You came to find me for more?" the man asked. He leaned against the wall and looked me up and down. His eyes raked me, devoured me as if I was a meal. He looked like a man who got what he wanted, took it.

I felt a wave of longing and loathing that wasn't mine. Whatever relationship these two had, it was complicated. It probably hadn't ended well.

I flashed a brief smile. "Always, but I need to eat first." It was a lie, but he didn't seem to realise. He appeared distracted.

I was relieved, sure he'd otherwise see guilt on my face.

He kissed my cheek. "Later then." He swept past me and out the door.

"Yes, later," I muttered to his back.

I was alone in the vast kitchen. I wasn't sure where it was in relation to the rest of the house. The rooms I saw so far seemed to be at the other end.

I grabbed a piece of fruit out of a bowl on a table

and bit into it. I couldn't taste it, but my host seemed to enjoy it. Juice dripped my chin. I wiped it off and opened the kitchen door.

Myrta's voice traveled up the corridor. I turned and walked the other way.

At the far end of the corridor was a workroom. The centre was dominated by a large table. An array of bottles covered the surface.

I paused on the threshold. It wasn't these which drew my eye.

On the far side of the room was a slender column of magic. It rose from a large glass sphere on a stand in the corner.

A hand clasped my throat from behind.

"You shouldn't be here," a voice growled in my ear. The man again. Was he following me?

"Raken." My voice trembled. "I was just curious. This great work we're undertaking—"

He squeezed slightly. "You have *one* job here, Daylia. To become pregnant. You're not here to think, or be curious."

I swallowed. "I'm sorry, Raken. I just—"

His grip tightened.

"I won't do it again." I was getting faint. "I swear. Please…"

"Please what?" he said in my ear. He pushed my

back against the wall and pressed himself against me.

"Please don't hurt me." I wanted to knee him in the balls. If I did, I'd be dead.

He looked me directly in the eyes, then stepped back and let me go. "Stay in your room," he snapped. "If Myrta caught you in here, she wouldn't be as gentle with you."

Gentle?

Whatever Daylia felt for him withered and died in those moments. Whoever this man had been, he was as much a monster as Myrta.

"Thank you, Raken." I forced an ingratiating smile. Daylia wasn't entirely cowed, but she was scared.

His hand brushed over my belly, a possessive gesture that made me want to punch him. As far as I was concerned, he had no right to this woman or any child she had. He was a parasite, feeding on her, using her for his pleasure and gain. If he hadn't died a thousand years ago, I might kill him myself.

"Go to your room. I'll be back later. I have important business to conduct first." He stepped back and gave her a push toward the door.

"Of course, Raken," I said meekly. "I look forward to it."

I wanted to be sick.

He murmured something in response and I hurried away.

I returned to my room and started to pack a bag. I didn't bother to fold anything, I just shoved it in and tied the top of the bag shut. I swung it over my shoulder when the door swung open.

Raken held a long knife in his hand. "Going somewhere?" He stepped forward and raised his arm.

I gasped and my eyes shot open. I was back in the present. Saff sat near me, his head cocked in concern.

"Are you all right, Summer?" he asked.

Daylia? I asked. *Are you here?*

A long silence fell, broken by a small, single voice. *I am here. You need to hurry.* She sounded choked. *There's not much time.*

He killed you?

You need to hurry, she sounded frantic.

You said that already. Did Raken kill you?

He killed me and my unborn child.

My breath caught in my throat.

"Summer?" Saff asked again.

"I need some air," I said and bolted for the door.

$\mathcal{I}$ ran straight into Kale, who must have been about to step inside. He grabbed me by the shoulders and pulled me to him.

"Summer, are you all right?" he rumbled. He sounded concerned, but being pressed against his hard body felt so good.

"People need to stop asking me that," I said to his chest. "I'm fine." More or less. I stayed pressed there until Zinnia loudly huffed. Reluctantly, I turned my face toward her, but stayed within his broad arms.

Zinnia looked at me down her nose, her expression unimpressed.

Undaunted, I returned her gaze until her eyes flicked downward.

She cleared her throat and fixed her eyes on mine again, less aggressive this time. "What's this about a key?" she asked coolly. "You were *supposed* to look for a portal."

I drew my face back from Kale and shot her an unapologetic look.

"Surprise," I said weakly. Now I knew for certain she wasn't Myrta, I gave her a watery smile. She might never talk about it, but she must have experienced the same horror of being trapped in her own body I had. The ability to see and hear everything, but not act on it. I'd never felt so powerless in my life and to be honest, I wouldn't wish it on anyone, even Zinnia. Not even Calla, who seemed ready to embrace the idea.

I glanced over my shoulder. "We should talk," I said softly.

She scowled. "I didn't come here to..." Her eyes shifted nervously.

"Yes, you did," I said. "You're not the monster here. Neither am I."

She licked her lips. "I don't think—"

"We need to work together," I said insistently. I silently begged her to agree. Gods, surely by now she understood what was at stake here.

Kale interrupted my thoughts. "Where are the others?" he asked.

"Kale!" Saff's voice behind me answered the question. "There you are, big guy."

Kale gave him a nod. "Here we are," he agreed. "We will work together. We must. Zinnia and I have reached an accord."

My heart stopped. I looked up at him. Did he really mean—

He smiled at me. "I told her everything. She agreed the realm is the priority. She's here to help."

I looked at her in surprise, but she gave me nothing in return but a slow blink. I sighed to myself. Of course she would help, but that didn't mean we were reconciled. Whatever it took, even if Kale had to be a go-between.

"Did you sleep with her?" Saff whispered loudly.

Zinnia turned pink and her expression became tight. "Where is my sister?" she asked. "My *other* sister," she corrected herself before I could protest.

"Inside." Saff jerked a thumb over his shoulder.

"I must speak to her," Zinnia declared. She swept past me and into the building.

"I did not have sex with her," Kale assured me. "She attempted to seduce me, but I had to decline. I explained my heart is with another." He gave me a soft smile.

"No wonder she's pissed off," Saff remarked.

I snorted softly. "That doesn't explain the other hundred and twenty-three years." I sighed and smiled back at Kale. "You really care about me?" I asked.

"I love you," he said gently. "I hope someday we can have some uninterrupted time together, so I can show you how I feel."

"I'd like that," I told him. I raised myself onto my toes and kissed his mouth. My tongue slipped inside. I wished we had time for more, partly because I wanted to and partly having witnessed Raken and Daylia having sex left me feeling twitchy as hells.

"Oh, look who finally showed up." Khat shoved himself into the space between our legs.

I had to cling to Kale to keep from falling backward onto my ass.

"You really need to stop doing that," I told Khat.

"Yeah, yeah. Are you here to stick your tongue down his throat or do you have something you need to do? You rushed off like you'd seen a ghost."

"Right," I agreed. "I'm surprised you noticed."

"I notice everything," he replied. "Don't let my innocent facade or relaxed personality fool you."

Saff choked back a laugh. "We're not fooled," he replied. "But the cat has a good point."

"Of course I do," Khat replied. "I always do."

"Me too," Saff smiled.

I rolled my eyes and peered down the length of the building. "It should be at the other end," I said without further explanation. I bit my lip and looked toward the doorway we'd just come from.

"Zinnia will keep Myrta and Calla busy," Saff said.

"Myrta is here?" Kale asked.

"In Tavar's body," I replied. "It's a long story. How did you know she wasn't in Zinnia when you told her everything?"

"I asked her if she knew a Fae named Cyrir," he replied. "She said she hadn't. I believed her."

"Calla would have," I said. Evidently she hadn't confided in Zinnia. Or if she had, Zinnia hadn't paid her any attention. For once, that might have worked in our favour. The gods know what she was telling Zinnia now. We'd probably wasted enough time as it was, we should get moving.

"Fletcher and Huon—" I started.

"Will keep them busy too," Saff said firmly. "Let's go wherever we're going."

I loved that neither of them had the foggiest idea

what I was going to do, but they had faith I could do it.

I nodded and dropped to a crouch. "We'll need to sneak under the windows." I would have shrunk, but that would make the distance further. I could grow into gigantic proportions and rip the place apart too, but I opted for subtlety.

At least for now. I wouldn't rule out blasting a few things later.

The guys lowered themselves behind me and we began to crawl.

I winced at the sound of the dry ground as it crunched under our ands and knees. There was nothing I could do about that, apart from move more slowly and skirt around the handful of dried leaves the breeze had blown against the wall.

"I don't know what we're doing, but I love this view of your ass," Saff whispered.

I stopped long enough to say, "Shhh," before I continued on.

"Sorry," he whispered.

I looked back over my shoulder and frowned.

He made a gesture to say he'd zip his lip and throw away the key.

I smiled, but nodded and turned away.

Khat sauntered past, his tail in the air. I thought

he'd make a snide remark, but for once he said nothing. His movements, usually fluid, looked as taut as my nerves. I trusted he would say something if he sensed anything, but his body language put me further on edge.

Daylia, are you there? I wondered at her name. It seemed sharing names with plants was a more modern thing for Fae, but her name was close to one. Rosette too. Perhaps Myrta was a long since extinct flower of some kind. One which smelled bad.

I am, she replied. *But the further from the key, the harder it becomes to communicate.*

She sounded distant, but audible enough for now.

You've waited a long time to be free of this burden, I said.

Perhaps a long time, perhaps a moment. I lost track after the ancients hid us away.

I suppose you would, I agreed. *Please don't tell me your child's soul was trapped too? Surely the ancients weren't that cruel?*

She went with the gods, Daylia replied. *She waits for me there, in their arms.*

Her tone made me want to cry, but I swallowed down the urge. *We will get you back to her,* I promised. If it was the last thing I did, Myrta would pay for all the pain she caused. Granted, the trolls wouldn't exist without her, but she was monstrous none-theless.

I believe you. She sounded so trusting I under-stood how she'd ended up in the situation she had. Myrta or Raken, maybe both, must have spun a web of pretty lies for her to get caught in. Maybe they told her she would save the Fae by having a child.

Where was Cyrir in all of this? I asked.

Daylia responded with a squeak and fell silent.

Gods, what had Cyrir done to her? In the back of my mind, I acknowledged that Raken might not have been the only one who tried to get her pregnant, but I suspected I would never know either way.

Sometimes the past had to remain in the past.

I'm sorry, I ventured, but she didn't respond. Hopefully I hadn't lost her entirely.

"Can we walk now?" Saff asked.

With a start, I realised we passed the windows where Myrta might have seen us and were almost to the rear of the building. Another door was set into the wall just ahead of us, identical to the others.

"I think so," I replied carefully. I glanced around. If Daffin and his trolls, or the silver Fae, had noticed us, I saw no sign. The silver Fae had probably hidden from Zinnia before she arrived. The trolls, she must have sent away, to keep them from overhearing. The idea made me furious. They were as much a part of all of this as the rest of us. They *should* be a part of it.

I pushed the thought from my mind for now and focused on the task at hand.

I rose slowly and froze, in case this end of the building was alarmed too. I didn't want to come all this way and die because I wasn't careful.

"Khat, can you feel anything off?" I asked.

"Only everything," he replied. "This whole place stinks of death and trolls."

"Apart from that?" I asked.

"Nothing specific," he confirmed. "But I'm not going through the next doorway first."

"Noted." I hadn't expected he would. I put a hand on the door, palm against the wood, and waited.

I didn't explode or disintegrate.

Yet.

I sucked in a breath and tried the knob. It didn't turn.

"It's locked," I said over my shoulder. I used a little magic to tease at the edges of the knob. I hoped to find a loose screw, or some other kind of flaw.

I didn't expect the knob to explode in a small, silent flash and send tiny pieces of wood in all directions.

"Oops." I waited a few moments, then pushed at the door. It swung open easily.

Mindful of Fletcher's warnings, I let the air escape before I stepped inside. The room was dusty, but unmistakable.

"This is the kitchen," I whispered. "Myrta's laboratory isn't far from here." That explained why Daylia had shown me so much of her memory. Familiarity with the place would help us navigate it more quickly.

"I should go first." Saff gestured toward the closed door which led from the room. Before I could protest, he was in the corridor.

A blast of magic shot toward him. It struck him squarely in the chest and knocked him backward. He flew several metres until he hit the wall with a thud. He slid to the floor like a doll made of cloth.

"Saff!" I called out. I started forward, but Kale grabbed my arm.

"I recommend caution." He loosened his grip and stepped ahead of me. He peered into the corridor.

I crouched low enough to look around his hip.

"I can't see anything," I said after a few moments.

"Neither can I," he agreed. "It may be that was the only magic trap. It may also be that there are more. Take great care."

I nodded and darted out to Saff.

He lay very, very still, his neck at an awkward angle.

"Saff?" I lowered myself to my knees beside him and touched his neck. "Saff? Please be alive."

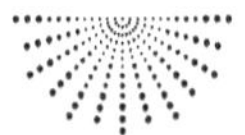

"Saff?" My heart in my mouth, I felt around his neck for a sign of his life's blood.

Nothing.

I swallowed back a sob.

"Saff? Oh gods, please…"

There, under my fingertips, a tiny flutter. Another.

"Thank the gods." I sniffed back tears. "He's alive, but weak. Khat, can you heal him? Please?"

Khat let out a gusty sigh and sauntered over to lick his face.

"He tastes salty," the mimicat complained.

Saff stirred.

"Just keep healing him," I begged, "please."

Khat grunted, but licked at Saff again.

My heart raced. The impact could well have broken things inside him we couldn't see. Parts of him which could stop at any moment.

I leaned in to whisper in his ear. "Please don't die. I need you. *We* need you."

"Who is 'we'?" Saff murmured weakly.

I laughed softly, relieved to hear his voice. "Everyone," I assured him. "Huon, Kale, Fletcher."

"Not me," Khat said. "I like you, but I don't *need* you."

Saff snorted, then groaned. "You like me?"

"Of *course* he likes you," I assured him. "You're very likeable. Loveable even."

Saff let out a long sigh and was still. For a moment I thought he was gone.

Tears welled in my eyes and a sob escaped my lips.

Saff's eyes popped open. "It's all right. I'm alive. Just resting my eyes for a moment."

"Oh, thank the gods!" I pressed my cheek against his. "You're lucky I won't sock you for scaring me like that. I might sock you later though."

"Go easy," he replied with a half laugh. "I'm going

to hurt for a while." Saff grimaced as Khat ticked at his other cheek. "Your tongue is rough, buddy."

"I can stop if you like," Khat said.

"I didn't say I didn't appreciate you healing me," Saff said quickly.

Khat's ears flicked back and forth, but he went back to work.

"Kale and you should look for Myrta's magic," he said. "I'll slow you down. I'll stay here and heal."

I hesitated. I didn't want to leave him, especially vulnerable as he was. Just because nothing else had attacked us in the last couple of minutes, didn't mean it wouldn't.

"Go on," Saff urged. "I'll be along in a minute." He smiled, but it looked more like a grimace. In spite of the healing, his eyes were full of pain.

"We'll be fine," Khat assured me. "I'll protect him."

What, with your razor sharp wit? I thought, but I said nothing. If not for him, Saff might have died. I'd have to make an effort to be nicer to him.

I glanced toward the door we'd come in through. No one came rushing in toward us, no army of souls or Zinnia's Fae. For the moment, everything seemed calm. For some reason, that put me more on edge.

"All right, but we'll be back in a few minutes."

Surely this wouldn't take any longer than that? I kissed the side of his mouth, careful not to touch anywhere Khat might have licked. I admired the mimicat, especially when he healed, but I doubted his saliva would taste nice.

Saff tried to nod, but only moved his head slightly. "Be careful."

"When am I not careful?" I asked with mock sweetness.

"Plenty of times." He squeezed my hand, then let it go.

I rose and gestured to Kale to stay behind me.

He smirked and fell into step next to me instead.

Slowly, we moved through the corridor. Our feet left prints in the dust before it settled behind us.

"It's just up here," I whispered. "Maybe you should go back and warn Huon to be ready to grab the key."

"He will know," Kale replied. "The souls will tell him, if the magic failing does not."

I nodded. "You're right, I don't want to put anyone else in danger."

"And yet, you're content to walk headfirst into it," he pointed out.

"I'm not sure I'd say I was content," I replied. "Maybe resigned would be a better word. Accepting. When Birch gave me this job, I couldn't refuse. He used some of his magic to bind me to the journey. I can't rest until it's done."

"Nor can the rest of us," he agreed. "We will see this to the end, whatever that may entail."

I glanced at him and wondered if there was some underlying meaning to his words. I saw nothing on his face but sincerity.

"We should be quiet," I said finally.

"Agreed."

I stepped on silent feet to the room Daylia had shown me. Between the memory and now, it didn't seem as though anything changed. The same bottles sat on the table, although they were empty now.

A layer of dust coated them and the tabletop.

The orb sat on the stand in the corner. Remarkably, it was clean. Not even so much as a mote of dust rested on its surface. Presumably the magic kept it from landing there. It would get dusty soon enough.

Daylia, are you here? I felt bad for asking. This place must hold so much anguish for her. She had been tied to it for far too long. The sooner we gave her some peace, the better.

I am here. She sounded clearer now than ever. *You are here.* She seemed pleased.

We are. Do I destroy the orb or just knock it off the stand?

I am unsure, she replied. *I think it must be destroyed, if it holds her magic.*

"Summer?" Kale gave me a questioning look.

"I'm talking to a soul," I explained. Briefly, I told him what she said, but left out the sex between her and Raken. "Do you think the orb is a conduit of some kind? I've never seen magic contained like that."

He scratched his head. "Neither have I," he agreed. "Perhaps we should attempt to break the flow first."

I eyed the orb dubiously. "When we tried to grab the key, it knocked us on our asses."

"Then we don't touch the magic." He looked around and picked up a bottle from the table.

Arm outstretched, he nudged the stand with the base of the bottle. The stand wobbled, but didn't fall. The flow of magic stayed steady the entire time.

He took a step closer and tried again. His hand came perilously close to the magic, but again the stand only wobbled.

"I suspect it's held there by the flow." Reluctantly, he replaced the bottle on the table and rubbed his chin.

"If nothing is a coincidence, then maybe the orb in my pocket would do something," I suggested. Before he could respond, I pulled it out and held it in the palm of my hand.

The glow of the magic shone on the surface of the small golden sphere. It highlighted the symbols etched in the side.

"Maybe if the right symbols were held the right way..." I mused. I rotated it slowly and watched for any change. Once I'd turned it far enough that I saw the first symbols again, I stopped and lowered my arm.

"Nothing. I don't want to think too hard, in case we get transported to the gods only know where." I put the sphere back into my pocket. "I guess we'll have to touch the magic." I grimaced.

"All right, but I'll do it," Kale said.

I put a hand up to stop him, but he lunged at the orb, fingers curled to grab it.

Time slowed.

I held my breath. Magic bathed his skin, turned his fingers golden. They all but disappeared into the flow as though he'd placed them in a waterfall.

His fingers tightened around the glass orb.

Every centimetre of his body lit up as though the fire poured into him and came out his skin.

Right before I started to think it was too much, and he might explode, he stepped back, orb in his hand. The magic winked out as if it had never existed.

Time resumed, but we stood still. The ground didn't shake beneath us. Between us we didn't take more than a breath or two.

"That was easy," I said tentatively. That in itself was as suspicious as fuck.

"Yes." Kale's eyes flicked back and forth as if he too was suspicious. "Very much so."

"Too much so?" I suggested.

"Perha—" His eyes widened. The orb dropped from his hands and fell to the floor where it shattered into a hundred pieces.

"Kale?" Then I felt it too.

The sensation of someone pushing themselves into my mind. I'd felt it before with Myrta, but this was different. Someone different.

What the fuck? Who the fuck?

It couldn't be.

Daylia?

She laughed softly and looked toward Kale through my eyes. "Did it work? Raken?"

Kale smiled slowly. "I believe it did, my love. We are restored at last."

Motherfucking gods! I exclaimed. *Raken? Are you nuts? After what he did to you? Why? We were trying to help you. To free you from the memories of this man. He murdered you, didn't he? You said—*

"That's right," Daylia said out loud. "He did. I have waited a long time for this."

This? I asked. *What is this?*

She raised her hands toward Kale and snarled. "For him to pay for what he did to me!" She released a bolt of magic.

Kale jumped aside at the last moment, but I was sure I would have smelt singed hair, if I had control of my nose.

Fucking hells.

Hey, I appreciate revenge as much as the next Fae, but you're in my body. Frankly, I'm getting tired of people thinking they can take over. I'm quite happy living in here, you know, alone. Well, happy apart from this whole revenge crap. And the whole key-finding thing. I'm really over all of that. I just want lesser magic back. Then we can get on with our lives. And I will get on with mine. But I can't do that if you get me killed. Or Kale.

Kale-Raken grabbed up the stand and threw it toward me—or Daylia. She stepped aside, into the path of a blast of magic aimed at my head.

Shit! I like my hair intact too!

"You can have your body back when he's dead," she growled.

"Daylia," Kale-Raken held up his hands in a conciliatory gesture. "Just think. Myrta will be pleased. With these bodies, we can retrieve the last key and get the dark artefacts back. After all this time, imagine the power we'll hold."

He gave a savage chuckle. "After a thousand years, we have won after all. These bodies are ours now. Fortunately for their former owners, their essence might survive for long enough for us to finish this task. They'll witness history. The making of a whole new realm. And other realms beyond this one. Realms where we will live as gods."

That was never Myrta's magic, was it? I asked. *The ancients left that there to keep you restrained.*

"And to keep the wrong Fae from getting the key," Daylia said.

Raken? I guessed.

Daylia sent another handful of magic toward Kale-Raken. He dropped to a crouch and it passed over his head and into the wall. It made a hole in the stone big enough I could walk through it.

A shout came from the other side.

Huon? I shouted, but the word didn't come.

Daylia, please don't kill the people I love. Not even Zinnia.

Kale-Raken rose to his feet. "It's time to finish this." The magic he sent toward us was twice the power of anything I had ever seen before.

Oh shit.

CHAPTER SIXTEEN

*D*aylia threw us through the hole my magic made. The blast hit just above my head, widening the hole significantly. We rolled and landed on our side.

Get up! I insisted.

"I'm trying." She grunted. "I'm not used to having a body." She heaved up and lurched a few steps before she turned and let off a shot of magic behind us.

It struck Kale-Raken, but only a glancing blow on his arm.

He sent more back, but less than before. Either he was beginning to tire, or he too struggled inside Kale's body.

Daylia tried to weave out of the way, but magic struck in the centre of our chest.

We were thrown backward and hit the ground with a hard thud.

For a long moment, I felt nothing. Then a wrench as Daylia was tossed out of my mind. That was followed immediately by all the pain which accompanied a hard landing. She'd shielded me from it, but now she was gone, leaving me to enjoy the trouble she'd created.

Lucky me.

Half a heartbeat later, I shrunk down to the size of Kale-Raken's finger to elude his next assault. That little, I had to use a small dose of magic to throw my voice.

"Daylia is gone, Raken. It's just me, Summer. I have my own body back. Can you please give Kale back his?"

He squinted. Sniffed the air. "She's gone," he echoed.

"Yes, her soul is with the gods now."

He grinned savagely, but lowered his hands.

Now I had my right mind back, I wondered how he'd used magic like that in the first place. Kale couldn't. He may have absorbed some when he grabbed the orb. If that was the case, it seemed to have worn off somewhat, after that big blast. That was fine with me. We didn't need an ancient Fae with that kind of power.

"So, about Kale's body…"

He turned and moved away from the hole and out of sight.

"I had a feeling you would say that." I took to the air, but kept to the walls and watched for him to come back.

"Summer?"

Saff's voice behind me made me startle so hard I flew into the wall face-first. I rubbed my nose and swore before I glanced behind me. He and Khat were crouched down low, eyes flicking this way and that.

Finally Saff spotted me and rose slowly. "Sorry, I wanted to be sure that was you."

"It's me now," I said, "but it's not Kale. We need to catch up with him and get Raken out before he gets back together with Myrta." While I spoke, I returned to my usual size. "How are you feeling?" I added and gave him an apologetic look for the afterthought.

He rolled his shoulders. "I've been worse. You?"

"Same." I nodded. "Same. When this is over I'm going to have a long bath."

"Can I join you?" He looked hopeful.

"Sure. You can rub my back." I smiled.

"Didn't you say we should hurry?" Khat asked irritably. "Let's just get the bloody key and get this over with."

If only it was as simple as he made it sound. I doubted it would be, it hadn't been yet.

I gave a quick nod and stepped through the hole in the wall. Rubble lay to either side and coated the floor for several metres. It crunched under my boots until I rose a handspan above it and flew instead.

"Might as well do this with some stealth," I whispered over my shoulder.

"I smell him," Khat said as we neared the kitchen. "He smells worse than Myrta."

"Oh good," I replied. "We've released an even bigger monster."

Saff put a hand on my shoulder to stop me. "This isn't your fault," he told me, his face insistent. "You were trying to get the last key. None of us could have known what they would pull."

I knew that, but I still felt as though I was an idiot for falling for it.

"Don't be stupid," Khat snapped. "The souls had to be freed. So assholes took advantage of that. Get over it and focus."

As pep talks went, it wasn't the warmest I ever heard, but it made sense.

"Khat is right," Saff said. "We had to do this either way. Now we'll just deal with—what did you say his name was—Raken? Him and Myrta. Look at everything we've done so far. This will be a breeze."

Breeze was accurate, as proven a moment later when a blast of magic flew past my right shoulder. Either he was a bad shot, or that was a warning.

His face appeared in the kitchen doorway. "Don't try to stop me," Kale-Raken growled. "I don't want to kill any of you, but I will."

"You don't?" Khat asked. "That's good to know."

"It really is," Saff agreed.

I bit my lip, then said, "Myrta does. She wants the realm destroyed so can start it all over again. She wants to be a god."

Kale-Raken's brow creased. "She cannot want that. We worked to create the trullen, for the betterment of Fae kind."

I remembered his contribution to the work and grimaced. "She does want that," I said. "She spent some time in my mind. I saw what she has planned. She admitted as much. She hates the trolls she created. She wants to kill them too."

His frown increased. "The trullen are our children." He sounded genuinely confused. "Daylia wanted to kill them, so I had to..." He swallowed audibly.

"Daylia knew it was wrong to create children to be used as slaves," I said as gently as I could. "But the trullen, they have thrived. They're free, and intelligent. It took us Fae a long time to realise that."

"Too long," Saff agreed.

"Don't get too sentimental, they still ate mimic-ats," Khat growled.

"They still don't deserve to die," I told Khat over my shoulder. "Nor do the Fae. That's what will happen if Myrta is allowed to follow her plans. You could help us stop her. It's not too late for that."

I held my breath and braced myself for him to attack. If he did, I would be ready with one of my own.

"If I don't help her, I die," he said finally.

"Isn't it time you went to your rest?" I asked. "You've been trapped here for so—"

"I'm not ready." He turned and disappeared into the kitchen. His footsteps headed toward the door and went outside.

"Shit," I said under my breath. I hurried after him, but kept my distance. If I attacked him, I might assume it would drive Raken out and leave Kale intact. On the other hand, I might be wrong and that would suck.

If he retaliated, I would die. That would also suck.

As Kale-Raken reached the other exterior door, he hissed.

I dropped to a crouch and gestured for Saff to do the same. "I think he's seen the silver Fae."

Where had they been anyway? That became evident when I scooted forward and a dozen silver-haired Fae stepped around the corner.

"I guess they went for reinforcements," Saff said.

"Why didn't I think of that?" I ran a hand over my head. "Oh yeah, our Fae still follow Zinnia."

"You dare to come to this place?" Kale-Raken railed at them.

"The silver Fae were exiled over a thousand years ago," Temara said coolly. "Much time has passed, enough to put aside the differences which drove us out."

"Exiled?" Saff whispered. "The plot thickens."

I bit back a laugh.

"You were exiled because of your failure to follow Myrta," Kale-Raken said. "Has that changed?"

I held my breath. I would really prefer not to have dragon shifter Fae on the enemy's side.

"It has not," Temara replied, her chin high. "When we learnt she still exists, we came to destroy her."

I let out my breath.

"We will destroy anyone who stands in our way," Kadagan said, his dark eyes piercing and cold.

I shivered. I wouldn't want him to look at me that way. When I thought about it, I didn't want him to look at Kale that way either.

Slowly, I rose, hands raised.

"My lover—" Was that the right term? Close enough. "His body is currently inhabited by an ancient soul. That of a man named Raken—"

Temara hissed and pulled out a knife. She lunged at Kale-Raken and slashed at his chest. She cut a slanting gash from his collarbone to his right pec.

He hissed in pain and fury. "You dare?"

Blood soaked his shirt in moments. Too much of it.

He snarled and blasted her, point blank, with magic. It took her in the chest and tore a hole right through her. She was dead before she hit the ground.

"This is bad," Saff remarked.

I had to agree. The silver Fae all snarled, their hands curled like claws.

"Please, it's not just Raken in there!" I called out.

The gods only knew what would happen if dragons tore him apart.

"His life is forfeit, along with Raken," Kadagan growled.

"Summer," Saff urged. "You have no choice."

"I know, I just…"

Kadagan began to shift.

I raised my hands and sent a shot of magic toward Kale-Raken. It struck him in the back. His body convulsed.

Kadagan held up a claw to stop his Fae from shifting further. "Wait," he ordered.

They waited.

I waited.

What looked like steam rose from Kale's chest.

"No!" he screamed. "I will not give up this—" The steam rose a little higher. It slowly formed into a ghostly face. A familiar one, handsome even now. I recognised him from Daylia's memory.

His mouth fell open in a silent scream.

"Raken. It's time to go."

He rose higher and arms joined his face. They scrabbled around in the air as if he reached for something to grab hold of.

"He's not going into anyone else," Saff observed.

"No," I replied, "he's not." I had a theory about that, but I would have to test it on Myrta first.

A torso followed, then legs. They kicked the air in obvious frustration, reminding me of a child having a tantrum because they couldn't get their way. He'd never get his way, not now.

Kale slumped to the ground beside Temara, leaving Raken to hover above him in despair.

He shook his ethereal head, but with each movement, he became more and more faint. Like a breeze dissipating smoke, his face dissolved. In a moment, it was gone. Then his chest and down his body.

The last piece of him left was a pair of feet which kicked at nothing, then they too were gone.

I sagged against the wall and took a few breaths. I had to compose myself before I was able to trot to Kale and drop to my knees beside him.

"Kale?" I touched his face. He was still breathing, but the gash in his chest looked nasty. "Khat, can you help please?"

The mimicat sighed. "You Fae need to stop getting injured," he complained. He slunk over and proceeded to lick Kale's other cheek.

While he worked, I looked up at the silver Fae. "I'm so sorry for what Raken did to Temara. You must know it was only him. Kale had nothing to do with her death."

Kadagan regarded me for a moment. I was halfway to thinking he was going to punish Kale, regardless, when he nodded.

"Very well. Our priority is Myrta," he said finally.

"That's funny, that's one of ours too," Saff said. "Go team."

I smiled at him, then turned my attention back to Kale. He stirred. His eyes flickered open. His gaze settled on my face and he smiled.

"You blasted me," he said weakly.

I grinned. "Sorry, it was that or let you be ripped to pieces by dragons."

"I prefer this," he agreed, "but my head aches."

I leaned in to kiss his forehead, then his mouth. His lips felt soft and warm. I could have stayed like that all day. "I'm glad you're alive."

"I am also glad of that," he agreed. He turned his face. "Thank you, Khat, I feel much better."

"You taste better than Saff," Khat said. "He's much too salty."

"That's not just my taste," Saff remarked. "I'm a salty bitch and proud of it."

I chuckled. "We should go inside." The gods only knew if the others were still alive and if Huon had the key yet. Anxiety blossomed in my chest and I swallowed hard.

"Yes, inside is good," Saff agreed.

"I give that a six, but I might give it more later, if this turns out all right," I said.

"I'll take it." Saff helped Kale to his feet and we headed back into the building.

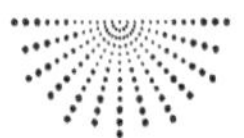

"Khat, where is Myrta?" I whispered.

"Still in the troll," he replied and went to lie beside Tiny.

Calla stood aside from Tavar and Zinnia and cast resentful looks in their direction every few seconds. Apparently she'd been pushed aside in favour of our older sister.

Could we use that somehow? I could try. Although, talking others into helping hadn't worked out so well yet.

Huon and Fletcher didn't seem to have moved from where I saw them last. The wall between the rooms was gone as if it was never there. Maybe it wasn't. It was possible none of this building was real, but an illusion created by magic. Sophisticated magic, but magic nonetheless.

Huon stood near the key and Fletcher was beside his brother. Both Rick and Jude were still encased in magic. Evidently that had nothing to do with the glass orb.

Well, fuck. That would have been nice and neat, but far too simple. I was starting to think the ancients had a sadistic streak.

Wait—I'd known that for a while now, I just didn't want to dwell on it too much. Truthfully if I met one I'd be torn between giving them a hug or a punch in the face. I would satisfy myself by ridding us all of Myrta.

"Summer, there you are," Huon remarked. "I was starting to worry." His expression was drawn, tense.

I doubt he'd *just* started to worry. He looked as though he'd done so since I ran from the room. Later, I'd praise him for staying put, near the key.

I raised my hands and offered him a smile. "I'm fine, more or less. In one piece at least." I shrugged one shoulder. "I had to take a detour to dispatch some friends of Myrta's." I turned my gaze toward her. "Daylia and Raken are gone. Moved on to the hells."

Myrta's face twitched with annoyance. She must

have expected them to join her at any moment. Maybe I should have pretended to be one of them, but it was too late for that.

Before she could respond, I continued, "I also brought some more friends." I gestured behind me as the silver Fae entered the room. Their faces were set like blocks of ice laced with grief for Temara. They wouldn't forget how she died, not for a long time.

I had a moment of satisfaction when Zinnia looked faint.

"Who… what… " She blinked several times.

"This is Kadagan, he's their leader." I hoped I had that right. I guessed Temara had led them until now, but the gods only knew if I was accurate. Whatever, it would do for now.

"You have no place here," Myrta said coldly. Her eyes were chips of stone.

"That's what Raken said," I replied easily. "It didn't work out well for him either."

Kadagan turned to me. "You vanquished Raken. Can you not do the same with Myrta?" He sounded as if he was discussing the pulling out of a weed from a rose garden, not killing an ancient evil.

"I will simply move to another body, and your troll will die." Myrta looked smug.

"I don't think so," I told her. "When I blasted Kale

here—" I nodded toward him, "Raken died. Same with Daylia. And Cyrir, come to think of it." I shrugged as if my heart wasn't racing. "All I need is a handful of magic and it's all over for you." I raised my arm.

Myrta raised hers. "My life is connected to those of your friends there." She nodded toward Jude and Rick. "If I die, so do they."

I glanced toward Fletcher, who was wide-eyed. Did I dare to call her bluff?

"What care do I have for two humans?" Kadagan asked.

"Can we stop with the bigotry?" I growled. "For the love of the gods, enough already. They are my *friends*. Hate on her, she's more or less evil." I waved toward Myrta. "But leave them out of it."

"My apologies." Kadagan gave me a shallow bow. "But they are a part of this, regardless, if their lives are tied to her."

"*If* being the word here," Huon said.

"You doubt the word of Lady Myrta?" Calla sounded outraged. Zinnia's presence hadn't deterred her entirely.

"Be quiet, Calla," Zinnia snapped. "You sound like an idiot."

Calla's face turned red and looked like she might

lash out at Zinnia. She spluttered for a moment, then fell silent.

I glanced sidelong at Huon "You think Myrta is bluffing?" I asked. "That Jude and Rick aren't connected to her?"

He shrugged. "If anyone would lie to save her ass, it would be her."

"We can't take the risk," Fletcher urged.

"We can't *not* take the risk," Huon replied. He gave Fletcher an apologetic look, but his chin was set firm. This was one of those moments where a king had to make a hard call, no matter what was lost in the process.

I swallowed and raised my hands.

Tavar's face contorted and the same blast of ghostly steam rose from the top of her head. It almost coalesced into Myrta's original face, but then it split down the middle.

Half sank back into Tavar, but the other half slammed into Calla and disappeared. She took a step back, eyes wide before the half of Myrta took control of her.

"That's a new one," I said in frustration.

"Yeah," Saff agreed. "One is the head-soul and the other is the ass-soul."

"I think they're both ass-souls," I replied. The

question was, could they act separately from each other?

Calla rolled her shoulders. "This Fae is nice and powerful," she said cheerfully. She turned to Tavar. "Maybe you should pick one of these, instead of that troll."

Tavar nodded. "I might just do that." Her eyes flicked back and forth and I knew the troll was still inside. Myrta's grip on her was weaker now she'd split in two.

I had a thought and frowned at Jude and Rick. They still hung there, eyes closed, faces pale. Every now and again, one would twitch, but that was the only sign they were still alive.

Without a word, I turned and blasted Tavar right in the centre of her chest. Her eyes opened wide, mouth formed an O. She flew back a few metres and landed hard.

Myrta's essence rushed out of her. Somehow Tavar managed to roll, jump to her feet and move clear.

"Zinnia!" I called out. I hoped like hells she'd be on the same page as me for once.

Without another word, we both turned our magic on the floating ghostly remains of a long dead Fae.

It stopped and quivered.

"No!" Calla shouted. From the corner of my eye, I saw her aim at Zinnia and let loose with a blast of her own.

Zinnia cried out in pain and her magic disappeared. A moment later, so did the half of Myrta.

Calla howled in rage.

The magic surrounding Jude and Rick disappeared. They both slumped, but Fletcher caught his brother and lowered him to the floor.

Huon lunged and grabbed the key before it fell to the ground.

I kept my eyes on Calla-Myrta and said, "Fletcher, is Rick all right?"

I was answered with a groan and Rick said, "What the fuck?"

"I'll take that as a yes," I said. "Jude?"

"I'm all right. I think," he said. He sat up and rubbed his head. Tiny bounded over to him and licked his face.

"Good, good," I nodded. "Fletcher, Saff, get them out of here. Tiny too."

For once, no one argued. They cleared the room. Huon and Kale arrayed themselves on either side of me. After a moment, Tavar joined them, her knife in her hand.

I heard the silver Fae spread out behind us.

"Is Zinnia…" I jerked my chin to where she lay on the ground.

"I don't think she made it," Huon said gently. "At least she was on our side at the end."

"Right." Too late for us to sit down and make amends over too much wine and hazelnut chocolate spread. She would have liked that stuff.

I pushed my regret aside and focused on Calla.

"That would make me the queen now," she stated. Nothing on her face suggested she fought against Myrta at all.

"Khat, is she still there?" I asked.

A flash of anger passed through her eyes. I didn't know if that came from my sister or Myrta. For some reason, that worried me most of all. Neither cared much for me, but Calla had years of research in her head, on top of Myrta's own.

"She's there. She's weak, but she's getting stronger," Khat replied.

I almost looked away from her. "How?" I asked.

Calla-Myrta smiled. "All that magic which was connected to me. I absorbed it again. Thank you. It will make me more powerful than ever."

I sighed dramatically. "It's over. Surely you realise that by now? You have no more moves to play. Our friends are free, you can't hold them over us anymore. You're outnumbered and we hold more power than you, no matter what you might have. We have all the keys. You've lost."

She smiled, a savage smile. "You'd let your sister die?"

"To save the realm, I would," I replied simply. "Calla would kill me to get what she wants. Whatever that is."

"You don't know?" Calla-Myrta asked.

I frowned. "Something about wanting the dark magic objects."

"Did she tell you why?"

I shrugged. "Why does anyone ever want dark power? Or any kind of power, for that matter? She was threatened by Zinnia. By me too, if she's to be believed. She seems to think the artefacts would change that."

"They would," Calla-Myrta agreed. "Infinite power. The power of the gods themselves."

"Who needs that kind of power?" Huon asked. "That's way too much, don't you think, Kale?"

"Indeed," Kale replied. "Far too much, especially for one person."

"That's your problem," Calla-Myrta sneered. "You think too small. You could have immortality. You could challenge the gods themselves. Create and destroy worlds."

"I don't want any of that," I replied. "No wonder the ancients buried them all."

"The ancients were as short-sighted as you were," she said with a tilt of her chin.

"Oh really?" I snorted. "And yet, here we are, ready to save the realm because of the clues they put in place for us, so long ago. They knew we would defeat you."

"Careful," Khat warned.

"What's wrong?" Huon asked.

"Her magic is building. Speaking of building, I'm getting out of this one."

"Nice segue," I said before he fled toward the door.

"Thanks," he called back, "I aim to impress."

I smirked.

"Give me the keys." Calla-Myrta held out her hand.

"Um," I said slowly, "how about no?"

"You don't even know how they work," she snapped.

"We'll figure it out," I assured her.

"If you won't give them to me, I'll have to take

them." She raised a hand and a fistful of magic flew toward me.

Tavar was ready. She jumped in front of me and deflected the magic with her knife. It bounced off the blade and over Calla-Myrta's shoulder. It slammed into the wall and left a hole which ran almost from the floor to the ceiling.

"Imagine how that will feel when it's you." Calla-Myrta smiled.

"No thanks." I sent a blast back, but she side-stepped and it passed out through the hole.

"Missed me," she said sweetly.

"Only this time," I replied. I sent another blast at the same time she did. The two balls of magic struck each other and exploded in a blinding ball of light. The backlash from it threw us all off our feet. I hit one of the silver Fae and landed on top of them.

"Sorry." I rolled off and Kadagan smiled at me.

"I'm happy to be of assistance," he said.

I grinned and jumped to my feet. "Where is she?"

I scanned the room, but Calla-Myrta was gone.

"Well, shit," I muttered.

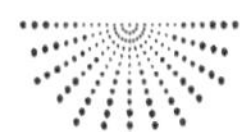

CHAPTER EIGHTEEN

"Half of you go out the door, the other half through the hole in the wall," Huon ordered. "Kale, Tavar: go with the first group and inform the other guys to keep an eye out for her. Tell them to get Jude and Rick clear. And Tiny."

Kale nodded and hurried out with the silver Fae.

He turned to me. "Summer, you and I are going through the hole."

I cocked my head at him and smiled.

"What?" he asked.

"You're hot when you get all kingly and leader-ish." I grinned.

He grinned back and gave me a gentle shove to follow the silver Fae. They piled eagerly out, even knowing the potential danger which may be on the other side.

I stepped through with my hands raised, ready to fire off magic at Myrta, whatever the form she might be in now.

I saw no sign of her outside the building. No Calla lying abandoned on the ground, no magic striking me or anyone else.

"No footprints proceeded us," the lead silver Fae said. He was a tall man, with his hair cut so short it was little more than a sheen on his head. Keen, dark eyes watched the area around us.

I flushed, embarrassed I hadn't thought about that myself. Thank the gods they'd had the presence of mind to check first.

"Thank you." Huon gave him a nod. If he was annoyed at himself for not thinking about footprints in the dust, no sign showed on his face. His resemblance to Birch in that moment made my heart ache. The late king would be proud of him, of all of us.

"We can act on two presumptions," Huon continued. "She shrank herself and flew out, or she went past us when our eyes were covered, and out the door."

"Or she died and we didn't see it," I said, unconvinced that was the case.

By the look on Huon's face, he didn't believe it either. He was gracious enough not to dismiss it entirely. "That's possible, but we'll act on the assumption she's still around, and be careful."

"All right." Perhaps I should refer to him as, 'your highness,' in front of the silver Fae, but we had no time for formalities. Plus, if I did that, he might think I should keep doing it, and I had no intention of that.

I kept my eyes open as we walked the length of the building and headed around toward the back. Everywhere I stepped was gravel and dust. It reminded me of our real priority—lesser magic. When we got it back, and we would, I would push for it to be renamed. If there was anything I had learnt from all of this, it was that there was nothing lesser about the magic which controlled nature. Blasting, shrinking, even healing—that was lesser than this.

We almost bumped into Saff and Kadagan as they came around a corner. Khat followed a metre behind. His tail whipped faster than I had ever seen it. I knew him well enough by now to know he was highly agitated.

"No sign of her?" Huon sounded disappointed.

"She's still here," Khat said, aggravated. "She won't

keep still long enough for me to find her, but she's moving west."

"West?" Huon echoed. "What's to the west?"

"The kitchen and other rooms," I said, distracted as my mind twisted and turned. "Where Kale, Saff and I dealt with Raken and Daylia." I shook my head. "Why would she stay here?"

"Maybe there's another source of power here she can draw on," Huon suggested.

I gaped at him, then turned and started off at a run.

"Summer!" Huon called out, but I didn't stop. I kept going, toward the door which led into the kitchen and left them all to run behind me.

I skidded into the kitchen and all but flew across and through the other door. I slowed and trotted down the corridor to the room at the end.

There, at the other end of the room, she stood. Calla's face looked sunken, but I saw Myrta in her eyes. So much of Myrta. Even at half of herself, she seemed to have overcome my sister entirely. Or maybe Calla surrendered. The idea made my heart ache for the second time in a few minutes. In spite of our differences, she was—had been—my sister.

I took a breath and resolved to mourn her later.

"There was more than the orb in here, wasn't

there?" I asked. More than the stand and the empty bottles. I eyed the table, but it just looked like a table. At this point, I wouldn't rule out anything.

She startled. Her head jerked up to face me. She scowled, but there was no hint of Calla, confirming my assumption she was gone.

"Little Fae." She spoke down the all-too familiar nose. "I built many secrets into this place," she replied proudly. "You think I'm beaten, but I have one more trick. One you couldn't have foreseen. One which will secure my victory."

"No offence," I said evenly, "but you sound like a madwoman." One who was unravelling fast. Maybe if I kept her talking long enough…

"Where are the other souls?" I asked. "All the other keys were protected by hundreds of them. This one only seemed to have two. Well, three if we count yours. And the other two were a bit nuts. All right, a lot nuts."

Her expression faltered.

"Orbs," I went on slowly and took a step toward her. "We've come across a couple of those on this journey. One here and the other on the island. You know all about the island, don't you? You followed us and grabbed Yina, Jude and Rick?"

"Naturally, I know," she replied with a sniff. She

looked as if she struggled to maintain control of herself. "That's why I'm here."

She held a hand over the shattered pieces of glass. Slowly, they drew closer to each other and began to bind together. Bit by bit, the orb started to reform.

I sensed if it did, that would be bad. I didn't know how, but bad.

"Do you know about the other orb?" I asked.

She faltered for a moment. Her eyes turned to me. "There is no—"

Without thinking, I reached into my pocket and pulled the orb forth.

She gaped and paled. "Where do you— How did you—"

"Oh, this little thing?" I tossed it up in the air and caught it. "The second key was inside it. Why, what does it matter?" The question was genuine. Apart from the golden sphere having been a container and opening a portal, I didn't know how it fit into any of this.

"Don't throw it," she insisted. "You might—" She stopped and clamped her teeth shut.

"I might what?" I asked. "Drop it?" I tossed it again.

"Yes, exactly," she snapped. "Are you young Fae really so ignorant, or just wilful?"

"A bit of both," I replied. "Why don't you enlighten me?" I rolled the orb around on my palm. Her gaze didn't waver from it the entire time.

"Give it to me," she said, her voice desperate, barely contained panic.

"You have your own," I told her sweetly. "One which will apparently let you win, remember? Is there a problem? Has something changed?"

She hissed. "I will *not* lose. I have worked for over a thousand years—"

"So, what would happen if I dropped it?" I threw it higher into the air this time. I barely caught it, but managed to grab it at the last moment.

"You fool," she growled. "You have no idea the power you're toying with."

"Oh, power you say?" I looked closely at the golden orb. A quick glance past it showed me the glass one was almost intact again. For some reason I knew whatever I was going to do, I needed to do it before that occurred.

"So, what happens if I press these symbols?" I poked at one shaped like a triangle, with my fingertip and waited. "Hmmm, nothing. That's underwhelming. What about this one? Still nothing." I was becoming frantic myself. The glass orb was at least three quarters formed.

I rotated the orb and saw a glint on one side. I stopped and peered more closely.

"What's this then?" I asked. "I've seen this symbol before. Let me think where." I looked at her over the small sphere. Her expression was one I hadn't seen on her before—fear. It sent chills through me. If anything could scare an ancient essence, then it must truly be terrifying.

And yet, I was as calm as a—something very calm. I couldn't think what now. I'd worry about that later.

"Oh, I remember," I said slowly. "I saw it in a book Calla showed me once, when we were children. It's the sign of the seven hells."

"No!" She started toward me.

I pressed the symbol.

CHAPTER NINETEEN

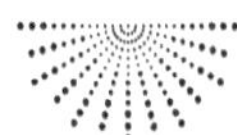

The sky turned black and filled with thunderclouds. That was weird, since I was inside.

Or at least, I had been, hadn't I?

I glanced from side to side. Still inside. Same room, same table, Myrta in my sister's body, her face contorted in fury.

My gaze inevitably turned upward again. The clouds rolled. Lightning flashed.

"Oh good," I said to myself, "I've opened a gate to the seven hells. What could go wrong?"

A face appeared in the clouds, ethereal like a soul. Clouds and lighting were visible through it.

I squinted. Was it a god I saw, or something else?

Whatever they were, they moved fast, closer and closer.

I put a hand up as though it might protect me from them and whatever they might do. At the very least, a god colliding with a Fae would hurt. Well, it would hurt *me*, maybe not the god.

"Summer?" The voice echoed as though they spoke through a tunnel.

Oh good, the gods of the lowest hell knew my name. That didn't bode well.

I lowered my arm and stared. Of course they knew my name, I knew theirs.

"Zinnia?"

She smiled. Just before she hit me, she veered to the right and zoomed past me, to Myrta. Slowly, Zinnia began to circle her. Myrta looked frantic. Her arms waved in the air as if to keep bugs from her face.

Zinnia was undeterred.

Confused, I watched for a few moments before my eyes were drawn upward again. Another face formed, then another. I recognised the next one as well, Temara. Daylia was next. Not, I noted, Raken. Perhaps the god of the lowest hell had other plans for him.

The troll who died when we first arrived joined

them, and Yina with her.

Others I didn't know joined them, until the cloud surrounded Myrta. Ghostly bodies joined the faces and hands reached out for Myrta.

"The god of the lowest hell says it's past time you joined him," Zinnia declared.

"No!" Myrta screamed so hard it must have made her throat raw. What was left of her essence started to rise up out of Calla's body. Hands grabbed for her, fingers twined and tugged her harder.

She struggled, writhing violently. She bared her teeth and growled in rage.

"No, you can't! I am a god—"

They gripped her harder, winding their essences around her like vines. Pinning her between them.

She screamed as she was torn free.

Calla's body slumped to the ground.

The air resounded with a sense of triumph. The souls rose and took her upward with them. All except Zinnia.

She looked down at Calla sadly, then to me.

"The god of the lowest hell will ensure Myrta pays for what she's done," she said. "The rest of us are free to move to the higher hells, to get some peace."

"Calla—" I started.

"Her soul is still in her body," Zinnia said. "Find

peace with each other. Tell her I loved her. I loved you too."

"I love—" Before I could finish speaking, she and the gate to the seven hells was gone.

"—you," I said softly.

"I love you too," Saff said from behind me.

I smiled and half turned around. "You saw all of that?" My hand closed around the golden orb. I tucked it back into my pocket.

"Yes, we were right here, but you seemed to have it under control." He put his arms around me and pulled me in for a hug. I leaned against him for a while, then drew back.

"I should see to Calla," I said regretfully.

He nodded. "I'll come too."

"All right, " I replied, "but I'm only going to the other side of the room."

He peered past me and nodded. "It's a long room," he said. "While I don't think you'll get into any trouble between here and there, I'm still coming. I mean, you never know."

"All right, I will appreciate the company." I smiled. Even though we were just been faced with the seven hells and the faces of lost friends and allies, we had time for some silliness.

"It's agreed then." He took my hand and we hurried over to Calla.

I dropped beside her and put a hand to her neck. Her life's blood was surprisingly strong in her veins.

"Calla?" I whispered. "Cal?" I hadn't called her that since we were children.

She stirred a little. "Sum?" she whispered. "I had the strangest dream."

"Oh boy," Saff whispered.

I murmured my agreement. When she opened her eyes and realised it was real...

Her eyelids fluttered. She looked up at my face. At Saff's. At the room around her.

"Oh." She closed her eyes again. "I wasn't dreaming."

"No," I said gently. "It's over. Myrta is gone. The ghosts of the past have gone to their rest."

"Zinnia?"

"Including her," I said.

"Ah." She swallowed audibly and looked up at me again. "I don't really want to be queen."

"That's good, I don't think Huon really wants to fight you." I glanced at where he stood a few metres away.

He smiled and nodded. "I really don't," he agreed.

"But it's not quite over. There's the little matter of the keys."

I flopped down onto my ass and sighed. "I know. I think we need to rest first though." The realm had suffered for long enough, but it could wait while we ate and slept. And I had some unfinished business with Kale.

"There's more." Huon crouched down beside us. "Calla, you seemed willing to serve Myrta."

Calla sat up slowly and watched him with wary eyes. "I was wrong. The books suggested she was a visionary, who wanted to save the Fae and make the perfect race. When she was in my head, all I knew was darkness. Twisted, corrupt darkness. I don't think she was sane."

"I'm not sure she was ever sane," I said dryly. "But there's still the matter of the artefacts. You were curious about them."

She licked her lips. "I still am," she admitted. "I want to see them." Before I could speak, she added. "I want to be sure they're not able to be used by anyone."

I searched her eyes, but saw only sincerity there. I didn't trust her, not yet, but I thought she wanted to do good, to atone for the past.

I glanced toward Huon. His expression was guarded, but he nodded.

"Very well then." He rubbed his chin. "We'll return to the capital first. I need to secure my throne and make sure I have a successor in place, in case we don't survive this last task."

"Huon—" I started.

"We can't predict what will happen," he said firmly. "The ancients needed a lot of sacrifices. They might require more. If so, we need to be ready. And for that, we need sleep and food. Lots of food."

"Food sounds good," Saff agreed.

"Fine." I got to my feet and offered a hand to Calla. She looked at it for a moment, then rose to her feet.

"Are you certain she is herself again?" Kadagan asked from the doorway.

I had forgotten about the silver Fae. They must have stayed back and watched the entire thing. He looked ready to shift and tear her head off, if necessary.

"Myrta is gone," I assured him. "She won't be coming back."

He looked as if he might not take my word for it, but he said, "That is fortunate."

"That's one word for it," Saff agreed.

"It is," Huon said. He gave Kadagan a bow. "On behalf of myself, as King of these Fae, I hereby cancel any exile imposed upon the silver Fae, and extend the hospitality of the capital. Uh, our capital that is. We have a lot to learn about each other."

Kadagan smiled. "We indeed have a capital, but we would like to accept the hospitality of the green Fae."

"Green Fae?" Saff asked, an eyebrow arched.

"You lived amongst the green in our day," Kadagan shrugged. "Perhaps that's changed?"

"Only in that the taint was killing all of the greenery," Huon told him. "I suppose it's accurate enough, but maybe we can just call each other Fae."

"That, perhaps, might take time." He cocked his head to one side and looked thoughtful. "I will address the matter with our new empress, when one is elected."

"Empress?" I echoed.

"Elected?" Huon asked. "We really do have a lot to learn about each other."

"That assumption seems correct," Kadagan said. "Let us begin now."

While they headed for the door, I stopped to look at the shards of the glass orb. It must have fallen apart again when the gate opened.

I stopped to pick up a piece which wasn't as sharp as the others. The rest would need to be cleaned up, but if a bit was missing, it could never be reformed.

I tucked it into my pocket beside the orb and hurried to catch up.

CHAPTER TWENTY

"This is nice." I kicked my legs and sipped my wine while I enjoyed the view. From the top of the canopy, the lights of the capital twinkled.

"It is," Kale agreed. "It seems as though we are the only ones who exist in the realm. Except the lights."

"Except those," I agreed. Somewhere down there, Huon talked with the other Fae, both from the capital and the newcomers. Since his arrival home, he had freed the trolls and insisted the Fae accept him as king. They all seemed relieved, if confused about his long absence.

He hadn't explained. He'd arranged food and accommodation, and this time away for Kale and I. I felt a little bad leaving him with the council and three overwhelmed humans, but before we snuck away, Saff ensured they were all at least three quarters drunk off their heads.

"When this is over," Kale said, "we should get more wine like this. Human realm wine, especially from Australia, is exceptionally good."

"It really is," I agreed. I licked my lips. I wanted to lick his. "Do you think we're far enough away from Khat?"

He chuckled softly. "I suspect the mimicat could climb up here if he wished. However, the last time I saw him, he was curled up with Tiny and was asleep."

"Oh good. Let's hope he stays that way." I turned my glass slowly with my fingertips.

"Indeed," he agreed.

"Um, this leaf is comfortable," I added. We'd shrunk down to fit without tipping it over. It wouldn't be a problem if we fell, our wings would catch us. If the wine bottle and glasses slipped off, that would suck. I doubted much human realm wine was left here in the Fae realm.

"Yes, it is," he agreed.

"Um." I couldn't think of what to say. We hadn't been alone like this before and it felt awkward. "You don't have to, you know."

"I don't?" He looked at me with amusement in his eyes.

"Of course you don't," I said quickly. Oh gods, maybe he really didn't want to. I flushed. What would I even do if he didn't? I could hardly seek out one of the other guys and say, "Hey, so Kale didn't feel like screwing, do you want to be his stand in?"

They were probably all as drunk as bats on over-ripe fruit anyway.

He took a breath and I braced myself for rejection.

"I have to tell you something," he said.

All right, here it came. He liked me, cared about me, but not like that. He just wanted to be friends. He was married. He preferred men. Gods, he might prefer mimicats for all I knew. They made for interesting conversation after all.

"Yes?" I said tentatively.

"Uh. I have never been with anyone," he admitted.

Fortunately I didn't have a mouthful of wine, or I would have spat it out.

"You haven't? Really?" I blinked at him a few times and tried to still my racing mind.

"Yes. I'm sorry, I'm not as exciting as the others. They would know how to please a woman, whereas

I..." He looked so dejected my heart melted a little more.

I put aside my wine and leaned over to kiss his mouth, lightly, gently, but with promise.

"I love you," I said softly. "Not because of your experience, but because of who you are. I want to make love to you." I liked the idea he had never been with anyone else. It meant we could explore all of the possibilities, together.

"If you want me," I added quickly.

"You're not deterred?" he asked.

"Not in the least." I placed my palms on his muscular chest.

"I'm relieved," he admitted. His voice was husky. "Can you teach me what to do? I have read several books, including novels, but I suspect the real thing is quite different."

"That's accurate." I started to undo the front of his shirt. "Novels are fantasy. This is real." I pushed his shirt off his shoulders and started to undo my own.

He watched me, eyes dark but soft. They widened slightly when I teased the fabric away from my breasts. He'd seen them bare before, but swimming was different to this.

This was for him.

I took his hands and pressed his palms to my nipples. His fingers closed on my breasts. He squeezed gently.

"I imagined how you might feel, but I was wrong," he whispered. "You feel so much better." He ran his hands over my skin, then took one nipple between his thumb and forefinger. He kneaded it with so much care I thought he was worried he would break me.

"Does that feel—nice?" he asked.

I swallowed back my desire, which threatened to rise too fast. "It feels very nice," I replied. I lay back and drew him down with me. The move dislodged his hand, but he replaced it with his mouth. His tongue flicked at my nipple while he sucked on it with soft warm lips.

"Gods, you learn quickly," I panted.

He chuckled, but didn't stop except to give attention to my other nipple.

How could I respond to that apart from undoing his pants and slipping my hand inside. I found his cock, thick, hot and hard. I stroked it lightly.

He broke off from what he was doing, to slide off his pants and carefully place them aside. Then he started on mine.

"Please tell me if I'm moving too fast, or getting too bold," he whispered.

"Oh, I will," I told him. At the moment he couldn't go quickly enough. I curled my hand around his cock and imagined him sliding it into me. My mouth went dry.

I raised my ass and then my feet so he could work my trousers the rest of the way off. He folded them quickly but neatly and placed them beside his.

He moved up beside me and ran a hand over one of my wings. His touch was almost enough to drive me over the edge, then and there.

"You have the most lovely wings I have ever seen," he said in awe.

I blushed. "No one has ever called them lovely before."

"Shame." He kissed my mouth. "You should be told every day how beautiful you are."

I paused and smiled. "You're right, I should." I was joking, but I didn't mind compliments here and there. "So should you."

He drew back and regarded me with amusement. "You think I'm beautiful?"

I smiled. "It seems like the right word. One of many. Handsome. Hot. Gorgeous…"

"You'll make me blush." He kissed my mouth, maybe to stop me from speaking.

That was fine with me. I traced the outline of his lips with my tongue. After a moment, his tentatively touched mine and stroked lightly.

I let my hand wander back to his cock and ran the back of my hand up and down his length.

He groaned. "I don't want to finish in your hand," he said breathlessly.

"In that case." We were moving quickly, but I was ready to feel him inside me. I moved my hand to his chest and hooked a leg over his hip. With a wriggle and a shift of my rear, I positioned my pussy in front of his tip.

"Gods…" He locked his eyes on mine and paused, and he knew he was savouring this moment.

I thought back to my first time, with Huon of all Fae. Nothing about that had been slow, or thoughtful. We'd teased and taunted for so long that when it happened it was frantic and over too soon. I was glad it wouldn't be like that with Kale.

He nudged my pussy, slipped the tip of his cock inside. Oh, so slowly, he slid deeper into me. Bit by bit I took all of him until he filled me completely.

"Summer," he breathed. "You feel so… I had no idea…"

"Mmmm," I agreed. "See, you're beautiful."

He chuckled softly and began to move slowly inside me. This was no frantic pounding, no fevered thrusting. Every movement was slow, calm, deliberate.

It drove me wild.

He cupped a breast with one of his large hands and massaged my nipple with the same steady rhythm.

"Gods," I breathed. "You're incredible." And he said he didn't know how to please a woman. Sure, there was a lot I could teach him and I looked forward to doing that, but this was exactly what I needed tonight.

The gods only knew what we'd face tomorrow and I wanted nothing more than to enjoy every moment and feel alive. Right now, I felt exhilaration in every nerve in my body.

"You are the incredible one," he said. "So beautiful, smart, generous, kind." He palmed my breast a little harder, then his hand wandered to stroke the edge of my wing.

A quiver went through me. "Oh, yes..." I whispered.

His thrusts became faster gradually. With each one, the pressure mounted inside me.

He rubbed my wing with the heel of his hand and that was it.

With a moan and a cry, an orgasm washed through from my core and outward to my hands and feet until they tingled and my vision swam.

Almost simultaneously, Kale grunted. He gave another thrust, then another and came, buried deep inside me. His whole body trembled and his eyelids fluttered shut for almost a full minute.

Then his body relaxed and he collapsed onto the leaf beside me. It bobbed before it rose again.

I unhooked my leg from over him and nestled into his side again.

"If we die tomorrow," I said softly, "I'm glad we got to do things tonight."

He kissed my forehead feather softly. "Agreed," he replied. "And no Khat."

"Yet." I picked up my head and looked around, but saw no sign of the mimicat. That was just as well. "He made the smart choice of staying away." I lowered my head again.

Kale snorted a laugh. "That is fortunate. I would not have wanted to miss this. Not for anything."

I licked my lips. "So, it doesn't bother you that I have Huon, Saff and Fletcher around too?"

"No," he replied without hesitation. "Does it bother you?"

"No. I didn't expect things to end up this way though."

"You didn't think four men would fall in love with you?" he asked.

"I'm surprised Huon and I didn't strangle each other," I said with a laugh. "Much less the rest of it. This whole journey has been a whirlwind, but I wouldn't change—well, most of it. Only those who didn't make it." Yina, Zinnia, the troll whose name I didn't know, and those long gone, but held in torturous limbo for so long.

I sighed. "I'm sorry, I didn't mean to bring it all up when we're enjoying such a good time."

He put an arm around me and drew me closer. "You wouldn't be you if you weren't worried about the others and the task we're involved in. Given the weight of the realm is on our shoulders, we can't put it out of our minds for long."

I exhaled through pursed lips. "This time tomorrow it might all be over." And it might not. The ancients could have thrown any number of extra obstacles in our path for shits and giggles. Nothing had been straightforward yet, there was no reason to assume it would be now.

In the back of my mind, I considered the thing we hadn't talked about, but we all knew we'd have to deal with. The dark magic artefacts. Releasing lesser magic might be easy compared with dealing with ancient objects of evil.

Gods, whatever could go wrong?

"We can do this," Kale whispered into my hair. "We *will* do this."

I hoped so, since we really didn't have a choice but to succeed. Failure was not an option.

CHAPTER TWENTY-ONE

"This is the place?" Rick asked.

"Yeah, it is." Fletcher looked tired and wary, but not as hungover as I might have expected. Rick looked somewhat bleary-eyed, as did Jude.

"Why are they even here?" Huon said into my ear.

"They insisted on coming," I replied. "They have been a part of this, pretty much from the beginning, especially Fletcher. It's their right to decide to come."

Huon huffed. "As king—"

"You're not their king," I reminded him.

He arched an eyebrow at me. "If Fletcher stays after this, I am."

"All the more reason he should be here then," I

said firmly. "Besides, are you going to take them back now?"

"No," he conceded. "Fine, they can stay, but Rick and Jude need to step back a safe distance."

I nodded my agreement to that. "Tiny as well." I would have liked to add Calla to that list. She looked far too excited for my liking. I was terrified. By now, she knew a bit about what our adventures were like. That should be enough to scare anyone.

"Yes, we can't let any harm come to the dog," Huon said.

"Someone needs to guard our backs," I added. "I keep expecting to see Myrta, or an army of the gods only know what."

He gave me a long, candid look. "Me too," he said softly. "I wonder if I should have brought all the Fae with us, to protect us from—whatever."

"We agreed the fewer people who saw the artefacts, the better," I reminded him.

"I know, I know." He sighed. "I'm second guessing."

"We should do this before you third guess then," I said as lightly as I could.

He grinned and gestured Saff and Kale over.

"We know Summer and Fletcher can pass through the trapdoor," he said. "So we each need to hold on to one or the other." He took my hand before anyone else could move. Kale took my other. Saff happily grabbed one of Fletcher's, and Tavar, her expression as unreadable as ever, took the other.

"What about me?" Calla asked. She frowned at the six of us, one after the other, then settled on me.

"Put a hand on my shoulder," I suggested. If it didn't work and she got left behind, then no harm done as far as I was concerned.

"Why don't we go through the gap we came out of?" Fletcher asked.

It was a good question, and one I had considered all morning. "If this doesn't work, we can try that, but the ancients have wanted us to use magic means to get around up until now. Using the symbol might —I don't know—announce our arrival in some way."

"If we sneak in, they might think we're not supposed to be there," Saff said.

"Something like that," I said. "But we're only theorising at this point."

Fletcher nodded. "Your theory makes sense. Why sneak when you can come with flair?" He wiggled his brows at me.

"I think that's a ten," I told him. "Why come unless you can do it with flair?"

Fletcher grinned from ear to ear. "Yes, finally a perfect score!"

Saff chuckled. "I'm a big fan of coming with flair."

"You're a big fan of coming, however you do it," I said with a knowing smile.

"You're correct," he said. "Same with you."

"Guilty." I smiled up at Kale, who had a smile at the corners of his mouth, and had done all morning.

He smiled back and squeezed my hand. "I understand this conversation is enjoyable, but I sense we're also putting off touching the trapdoor."

"Guilty again," I admitted. I looked over to Fletcher. "Are you sure you want to go back in there?"

He twitched as though he'd rub his chin if his hands were free. "I want to. I need to. If only to assure myself I can leave again." A flash of fear passed though his eyes and I understood. If he was somehow left alone, with no Fae to get him out, he would spend the rest of his days back in there.

"We will *not* leave you in there," Saff assured him.

"Right," Huon agreed. "We will all get out, even if we can't get at the lesser magic."

"Agreed," Kale said. "No one will be left behind."

Tavar inclined her head slightly.

"This is all nice and sentimental," Khat said, "but

can we just get on with this?" He slunk toward me and pressed himself against my leg.

"You're coming with us?" I asked him.

"Someone has to keep you out of trouble," he replied.

"And who will keep you out of trouble?" Saff asked.

"Me, myself and I," Khat said firmly.

"All right, we should do this before we end up with a dozen of us." Before anyone else could speak, I said, "There's not that much room in there."

I stepped forward, toward the trapdoor and lowered a hand toward the symbol. It looked harmless, shining there in the morning sun. Where before it was surrounded by grass, it now stood alone in a desolate field. The stark surroundings served as a reminder of all that was at stake.

My hand still in Huon's, I raised my pointer finger and touched the symbol.

For a moment, nothing happened, then we were pulled down, sucked as though through a straw. Huon let out a cry of surprise. Kale's hand tightened around mine.

I felt as if my head was being pressed from all sides. The sensation passed through me, down to my toes.

Then we were tossed into darkness.

I immediately let go of Huon's hand and made a ball of light to balance on my open palm.

Even knowing where I was and that I could leave, my stomach heaved at being back here again. The first time, I had no idea what happened and if I was still alive. Fletcher and I had scared each other. I couldn't even grasp being down here as long as he was.

Just as I thought that, he appeared, Saff and Tavar in tow. He flinched, but Saff made light with one hand and gave him a hug with his spare arm.

Fletcher smiled faintly. "Thanks, buddy."

"Any time, buddy."

"So, this is the place." Calla sounded intrigued.

"Your powers of observation are astonishing," Khat told her. Since he hadn't hissed, I assumed all trace of Myrta really was gone. A tiny bit of doubt had persisted in the back of my mind.

All of us Fae had light burning now, so the whole tunnel was well-lit.

"It looks like the one on the island," Huon said. "Same kind of stone and all that."

"It does," I agreed. "I hadn't really noticed the first time."

I moved over closer to Fletcher and wound an arm through his. "Are you all right?" I asked softly.

He hesitated. His lips moved a few times before any words came out. "It doesn't seem like the same place. I couldn't see it until you got here. The smell, though, it is the same."

I sniffed. Dank and damp. "You're right, it is. There's probably more mushrooms now, if you want some."

He looked at me in surprise and then laughed. The sound echoed through the tunnel. "I never want to see another mushroom as long as I live, much less eat one."

I grinned. "I thought not. They're definitely not as good as the hazelnut chocolate spread in the human realm."

"Or coffee," he agreed. "The beer is good here though." He rubbed his head. "Maybe not so much next time."

"If my stomach wasn't churning with nerves, I might be hungry after all this talk of food," I said.

"Me too." He leaned in to kiss my mouth. "You taste the best of all of those things anyway."

I smiled and kissed him back. "You're not so bad yourself."

"Good to know," he said.

"Hey, you two," Huon called out. "Which way to the door?"

I glanced around to get my bearings again. "We went downward."

Fletcher nodded. "Right, we did. Down the steps."

"Steps, got it." Huon gestured for us all to move into line behind him, and started through the tunnel, toward the door.

For some reason, I'd half expected things to look different in here. For all I knew, the whole thing could have caved in at some point over the last five years. Instead, it looked as if we'd just left. I searched, but found no footprints in the dust. Otherwise, nothing changed.

"Fascinating," Calla said from behind me. "This must have been part of an ancient city. There might be corridor upon corridor, just waiting to be excavated. Imagine the treasures of the past we might find buried here."

"I've seen enough *treasures of the past* to last me a lifetime," I said over my shoulder. "Especially the ones we've met along the way."

"I'm all for studying the past," Huon said, "but this is best left undisturbed."

Calla huffed. That was an argument for another day.

My heart raced harder and harder as we descended the steps deeper into the heart of the tunnels. I kept expecting something to jump out at us, or for the steps to turn into a slide. Maybe when we reached the bottom, the door would be gone, replaced by a gate to the hells, or just a wall.

Maybe, maybe, maybe. My head spun with possibilities until a dull ache settled in my temples.

I rubbed at them and almost missed when Huon stopped. I caught myself before I ran into his back, and dropped my hands.

"The door," he stated.

"It is indeed a door," Saff agreed.

"Look at you two, being all obvious," Khat said. "It's not just a door. There's a butt load of darkness on the other side of it."

"We already knew that," I told him. My gaze found Calla. I was ready in case she tried to pull anything, but that made my head ache all the more.

"There's only one keyhole," Huon said.

"We knew that already too," I said. That had been at the back of my mind, along with everything else. "Three keys, one hole."

"The irony," Khat remarked and looked pointedly at me.

I rolled my eyes. "Your disapproval is noted, but ignored. Besides, there's four of them."

"Whatever." He flicked his tail and went to stand beside the door. He rubbed his face against it, then slunk away. "The lesser magic is still inside. The door itself seems harmless. And for the record, I deserve a score for that innuendo."

"I give it a nine, but what do you mean by *seems?*" Saff asked.

"I mean *seems,*" Khat said. "It's not made of dark magic and it doesn't contain the soul of Myrta. Apart from that, you'll have to figure it out."

"There's only one way to go about this," Huon said, as though Khat hadn't spoken at all. "We try one key at a time. One will have to work."

"That must have been exhausting," Khat said.

"I beg your pardon?" Huon asked.

"It's about time someone did," Khat said. "I was referring to you jumping to conclusions."

"You have a better idea?" Huon sounded irritated.

"No, but these were the ancients. I would bet all the tuna in the human realm they have more surprises planned for us."

"I wouldn't take that bet," Huon said. "They more than likely do. In the meantime, we have a door and keys, and need to try something."

"I will try first," Kale said. "Mine was the first key."

"I feel as though I should argue and tell you to step aside," Huon said. He ran a hand over his hair. "It might have been first for a reason, so it makes sense to try that first."

"Indeed." Kale agreed.

I swallowed hard. "Please be careful."

Kale turned to kiss me, long and soft on my mouth. "I will always be careful," he assured me.

"You had better," I growled. "All of you."

"You too," Huon told me.

I held my breath while Kale pulled the key from his pocket and slid it into the lock.

CHAPTER TWENTY-TWO

"Well, we should have expected that," Saff said.

"Yes, I suppose we should," Huon agreed.

I muttered my agreement.

Kale twisted the key again and pressed the door with his palm. It still didn't open. He withdrew the key and stepped aside.

"My turn." I pulled out my key and walked forward. I touched the door with my fingertips. Khat said lesser magic was there, on the other side, but I couldn't feel anything but the wood under my skin. The fact the door survived this long intact confirmed there was some kind of magic lurking here. Hopefully just benign.

I wouldn't rule out the idea that dark magic kept

the wood from crumbling, but I pushed that out of my mind for now.

I held the key between my thumb and forefinger and tried it in the lock. As Kale's had, it slid in easily, but refused to turn. I twisted it the other way, but it wouldn't budge.

I pulled it back out and shrugged. "Huon, try yours."

"You look disappointed it's not yours," he told me. He put a hand on my shoulder, his head tilted.

I gave him a lopsided half-smile. "I am, but I'm just as disappointed Kale's key didn't work either. If yours doesn't, then—"

"It will," he assured me. "We haven't come all this way only to fail." He put a finger under my chin and raised it up to look him in the eyes. "All right?"

"I know," I assured him. "We've got this. Go ahead and try."

He kissed me lightly, then pulled out his key with a flourish. He approached the door with exaggerated swagger which made us all chuckle. He slipped the key into the lock and twisted it. The door stayed shut.

"Fuck."

He turned it the other way.

"Double fuck."

Shoulders sagged, he pulled the key free and looked as if he might throw it on the ground in disgust.

"What now?" Fletcher asked.

I ran a hand over my hair. "I hope there are no gods up there in the seven hells laughing at us for running around to get these keys for nothing."

Saff rubbed his chin. "For so much of this," he said slowly, "we've had to join together for things. Maybe we need to do that again now."

"How?" Huon asked. "Join hands while we try each key?"

"Sure," Saff replied. "Why not? It wouldn't be the strangest thing we've ever done."

"That's true," Huon admitted. "It might be better to try that before we ask Summer and Calla to blast the door down."

Calla looked pale at the suggestion, but I was all for it. I'd had enough of this wild goose chase. Although, if that was all it took, we could have had this over with days ago, and without anyone having to die.

"Wait," Fletcher said. "I don't think it's us who are supposed to join together this time."

I arched an eyebrow at him in question. "What do you mean?"

He scratched at the scars on the side of his face. "What if the keys are supposed to merge together somehow? To make one key to open the lock."

"Still not the strangest thing we've done," Saff said.

"It's worth a try, I suppose." I held out mine on my palm. Kale lay his across it.

Huon looked thoughtful for a moment, tentative. "If the keys bind together and still don't work—"

"Then I'll blast the door down," I assured him.

He set his mouth in a resigned line, then placed his key on the top.

We waited.

And waited.

I sighed. "You know what I'd like to have happen?"

"What?" Saff asked.

"*Anything*. All of this nothing is driving me crazy." After a beat I added, "All right, crazier."

I shook my head. "Calla, Tavar, was there anything in all of those books or legends which mentioned keys, or what we're supposed to do with them?"

"Nothing which I can recall," Tavar said. She reclined against the wall, knife in hand. "Just that they had to be found."

I nodded and turned my gaze toward Calla.

She swallowed audibly. "Only the last key being in the heart of the taint," she replied slowly.

"Heart of the taint," I echoed. I sat down on the floor, crossed my legs and stared at the keys. "Heart… hearts are the middle of things. The middle of people—sort of. The centre. What else is at the centre of anything?"I clicked my fingers. "We are. We're at the centre of all of this."

"Summer?" Huon crouched beside me. "What are you getting at?"

"The Fae realm, the human realm, the seven hells, we're at the centre of all of it. And what got us here?"

"Our wings?" he asked.

"Our feet?" Saff guessed.

"The ancients and their screwed up idea of fun?" Khat suggested.

"The portals?" Fletcher asked.

I pointed toward Fletcher. "You're the closest." I drew the golden orb out of my pocket. "This. It opened a portal, opened a gate and held the middle key."

I dug my nail into the side of the orb and it clicked open. My heart raced. I had no idea if this would work or not, but something inside me told me it would.

I tipped the hand which held the keys and they tumbled into the middle of the orb, one on top of the other.

The moment they touched, magic flashed so brightly I had to half-close the orb to avoid being blinded.

Then the flash was gone, replaced by the smell of burning.

I held my breath and eased the orb open again. There, in place of the three silver keys, was a shining golden one.

"Either this will open the door, or I've fucked up badly," I declared.

Huon grinned. The look faded. "I don't feel the key now."

I blinked. "You're right, neither do I."

"I also do not," Kale confirmed.

"Um." Saff raised his hand. "I think I do. It's pulling me over like when I was drawn to Summer." His eyes were wide open in amazement. "Not that I'm not still drawn to Summer, but this is different. I mean—" He flushed.

Huon chuckled. "We get it. Are you going to take the key, or just stand there and babble like a confused child?"

"You don't like my babbling?" Saff pretended to be offended.

"I like it fine, but we all agreed we wanted to get on with this." Huon poked him in the hip with a fingertip.

"Oh, right. It's not going to bite me, is it?" Saff eyed the key doubtfully.

"I don't believe any of us have been bitten by any keys," I replied. "Yet."

"You'll be bitten by a mimicat if you don't hurry up," Khat growled. His tail swished against Saff's leg.

Saff smirked and leaned forward to pick up the key. This time I was relieved when nothing happened.

"It feels warm," he marvelled.

"It would," I said, "it just got made."

"A newly forged key of gold," Kale whispered.

"What?" I asked him. "Was that something you read somewhere?"

He smiled. "Indeed not. It's something I will write when I tell the story of our adventures."

"You're going to write a book about us?" I asked.

"Why would I not? Our descendants will want to know what we did here."

"If I may," Calla said tentatively. "I should like to help you write it. I think I have some insight to add."

Kale inclined his head. "Indeed, I will need assistance from everyone."

Calla beamed and rubbed her hands together. "We could call it—"

Huon cleared his throat. "Can we save the realm first? Then you can think up a book title."

"Right." Calla's face fell, but she still looked excited.

"All right, here we go then." Saff stepped over to the door and slid the key into the lock. "It went in."

"Of course it did, it's the same size as the other three," Huon said.

"You'd think something made from three keys would be bigger," Saff pointed out.

"It's best not to question magic too much," I said. "Does it turn though?"

Saff made a face. "I suppose I should try. Should we hold hands or something?"

"It can't hurt," Huon agreed.

"You hope," Khat remarked.

"Unless you have something helpful to add, maybe you can shut up," Huon told him.

Khat rolled his ears back and forth. Finally he lay down against the wall and proceeded to lick his private parts.

"I think you've been told," I said to Huon and smiled sweetly.

He smirked and shook his head. He took my hand and one of Saff's. I grabbed Kale's as he took Fletcher's. Calla eyed him dubiously before she joined the end of our chain.

"Tavar?" I asked.

"I'll stay here and watch your backs," she said. "If I'm meant to be there to help, I'll get sucked back in again."

"That's true," I replied. She was sucked into the human realm, after all.

"All right, are we all ready?" Saff asked.

"Wait," Huon said suddenly. He let go of my hand and scratched the side of his nose. "Ah, that's better."

He took my hand again while I laughed softly.

"What?" he asked. "I don't want to risk being sucked into a portal with an itchy nose."

"Fair enough." I smiled and stood still, my heart in my throat.

"Here we go." Saff turned the key.

The click as the lock opened was loud enough to echo through the tunnel.

Saff pressed his palm to the door and pushed on it.

The door swung inward without a sound, as if it was recently oiled.

"We should step back," Fletcher reminded us.

We did, but only shuffled a few steps. I pressed myself against the wall and strained to see inside. I couldn't make out a thing, it was pitch black.

I drew my lip between my teeth. "How long do we have to wait?" I asked.

"What is that?" Saff called out in alarm.

"What? Where?" I squinted, but had no idea what he was referring to.

"There, at the bottom, left corner of the doorway."

I strained and finally made out a slight glow.

Soft.

Green.

Growing.

"Lesser magic," I whispered. "I mean, *nature* magic." There was nothing lesser about this. It was beautiful. I felt its healing power from here.

"Oh my gods," Huon breathed. "We did it. We freed the magic."

A whisker of green turned into a thicker strand, which doubled in the blink of an eye, and then doubled again. It slipped over the threshold and stopped.

A section of the magic at the front rose, as though it was looking around, assessing whether or not it was safe to keep going.

"Is it—sniffing the air?" Saff asked in wonder.

It certainly did seem to be doing that.

"It's all right," I told it gently. "You're free now. Go and…help the realm." For a moment, I thought it might refuse and retreat back into the darkness.

Instead, it slithered toward the stairs and started upward. It grew as it went, like a vine of magic.

"Well, thank the gods for that," Saff said, breathless as though he too had held his breath for the last minute or so.

"Now for the hard part," Huon said. "We have to go inside and deal with the dark magic artefacts."

"Hey," Fletcher said. "Where is Calla?"

I groaned. "I bet she went in ahead of us." Of course she betrayed me. I'd expected her to, but I had been halfway to thinking maybe she wouldn't after all.

I squared my shoulders and, careful not to tread on the ever increasing flow of magic, stepped into the darkness.

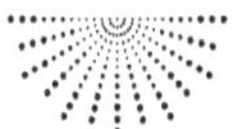

The moment I crossed the threshold, the room beyond became bathed in light. It wasn't sunlight, or even the green glow of natural magic as it bled from the room. No, this was a sickly yellow-brown light, as if formed by the taint itself. The air stank, that same rotten smell of dying trees, or off meat.

I took shallow breaths and tried to still my stomach.

"Calla?" At first I saw no sign of her.

When I'd imagined dark artefacts, I hadn't pictured anything like these. A sword with a blade so dark no light reflected from it, hung on one wall. On another hung a mirror. It too, reflected no light. When I stepped closer to peer into it, I saw no reflection, only a swirling cloud of yellow-brown light and blackness. I had the feeling if I stared into it for long enough, I might be drawn into it forever.

Beside the mirror, a shelf held a circlet, plain and apparently made of silver. If this was anywhere else, I might have tried it on. Here, it would probably claim my soul and turn me evil.

It was too early in the day for that.

"Calla?" I called again. "I know you're in here."

"Summer?" Huon's voice at my shoulder made me jump.

"Gods!" I pressed a hand to my pounding heart. "You scared the crap out of me.

"Sorry," he said, his voice low. "This place is creepy as hells, but none of this looks—dangerous. I was expecting it to jump out at us or something."

"Just because it hasn't, doesn't mean it won't," I said dryly. Now I would be looking for just that to happen.

"I've always wanted a sword like that," Saff remarked. He pointed toward the one on the wall and in the next moment it was in his hand.

"You were saying?" I said to Huon. "How many times have I said not to say things like that?"

He held his hands up. "Sorry. Hey Saff, put the sword down."

"Saff is no longer here," Saff said, his voice deeper than usual. "He is gone. I have taken his place. You may call me—"

"Saff, stop being a dick and put the swords down," Huon told him.

Saff grinned. "Sorry, I couldn't resist."

"I'm sure you could if you tried hard enough," I told him.

"Yeah, maybe." He replaced the sword in its bracket on the wall.

"How did you do that anyway?" Fletcher asked. "Just so I don't do it by accident," he added quickly.

"I just put my hand up and thought how much I wanted it," Saff said. He had the sense not to demonstrate it a second time. He cocked his head. "Summer, where did you get the circlet from?"

"I beg your—" I put a hand to my brow. A glance toward the shelf showed a space where the circlet had been. I took it off my head and frowned at it. "I did think how pretty it was," I said slowly.

I put it back on the shelf and stepped back.

"It's like a pixel," Fletcher remarked.

"A what?" Huon asked.

"A pixel," Fletcher repeated. "It's a computer program which tracks what you look at on the internet and then you get sent ads for the things you just looked at. Some people swear they only have to think about an item and they get ads for it."

"So maybe this dark magic reads our minds and gives us what we want?" I said. "In that case, hot coffee and hazelnut chocolate spread." I held out my hand.

Neither appeared.

"Just as well, I probably shouldn't drink coffee created by dark magic."

"That sounds like good advice," Huon agreed.

"What about beer?" Saff asked.

"Are you likely to come across beer created by dark magic?" I asked.

"Come across it? No," Saff replied. "Find some? You never know."

I snorted in reply. Trust him to turn it into something sexual. Not that I minded, it took the edge off the pressure. Or added to it, depending what kind of *pressure* was involved.

"I still wouldn't drink it," I said.

"I would certainly advise against touching anything here, much less eating or drinking anything you find, or wish up," Kale said. "Dark magic is strong and deceptive."

"Unless it's deceiving me now, my sister isn't here," I said. I'd reached the centre of the room.

From here, I could see all four of the walls and several artefacts I hadn't noticed at first. One looked like a mask from a masquerade, while the other seemed like nothing more sinister than an old book. I'd bet it was full of horrible ways to do nasty things to otherwise innocent Fae.

"No souls either," Huon said. "I would have expected something to be defending this place."

I frowned. "You're right. Unless we haven't seen it."

"Um, Summer," Fletcher said. He pointed at the wall behind me.

I spun, expecting to see something about to attack me.

Instead, I saw the mirror I'd first seen when I'd entered the room. Inside the mirror, within its beveled edges, was my sister.

She stared out at me, eyes wide. Her arms flailed. Her mouth opened in a silent scream.

"I'm going to make a wild guess here—she didn't desire to be inside that mirror," Saff said.

"It's likely she wanted the mirror," Kale said.

I glanced back at him. "Why? What does it do?"

He shook his head. "I don't know."

"We can't leave her there," I said, my voice high.

"Can't we?" Huon asked.

I blinked at him and started to prepare an angry retort.

He held up his hand. "She knew the danger and still snuck past us to come in here. Even if we knew how to get her out, I can't risk—"

"We have to try," I insisted. "If you won't, I will." The problem was, I didn't know how. I didn't particularly want to risk being sucked into it myself.

I chewed my lip. I had an idea, but only the gods knew if it would work or not.

"Summer—"

I felt someone's fingers close around my arm at the same moment I reached for the mirror.

I felt a wrench which made me cry out in surprise.

Then I was surrounded by brown-yellow clouds, swirling amongst black.

I'm inside a dark magic mirror. Fuck. This is a new low.

"I don't know if this is cool, or if I should be scared," Saff said, his eyes wide.

I rounded on him. "Saff? Why the hells did you let yourself be dragged into this?"

"I wasn't letting you come alone," he protested. He opened his mouth as if to add more, but I cut him off.

I shook my finger at him. "This is no time for innuendoes. We need to find Calla and get the hells out of here."

"Right." He looked serious, but I suspected it wouldn't last for long. Hopefully he could hold it together long enough for us to do this.

"All right, how big can the inside of a mirror be?" I asked.

"It depends, is this an actual mirror, or somewhere else? One of the hells maybe?" He turned around slowly.

I shook my head. "I have no idea, but I presume it's not just a mirror." I looked the way we'd come and saw Kale, Fletcher and Huon's worried faces looking inward at us. I gave them a wave to reassure them we were fine.

They didn't look convinced.

I forced myself to turn away. "Why would anyone come here?" I asked, half to myself.

"That depends, where is here?" Saff asked.

I ran a hand over my hair. "It looks as though we're inside dark magic," I said slowly.

"I think this might qualify as the strangest thing we've done," Saff said.

I snorted. "Yes, it would seem so. Maybe she thought she could absorb it somehow."

"Why?" he asked.

I chewed my lip and shook my head. "I don't know that either." I turned a slow circle. "Calla? Where are you?"

As if wishing made her appear, she was suddenly in front of me.

"Summer?" She reached out toward my face.

"Calla?" I grabbed her wrist. "What the hells are you doing?"

Her face looked haunted. "The mirror. It was supposed to…" Her eyes were wild.

"Supposed to what?" I demanded. "What does it do?"

"Heart's desire," she said. "It was supposed to give me my heart's desire."

I shook my head. "What is that? Please don't tell me you wanted something silly?"

"I wanted… I wanted…"

"You wanted what?" I felt like grabbing her by the shoulders and shaking her. I didn't, but my hand tightened around her wrist.

"I wanted to be appreciated," she said finally.

"You are appreciated, you bloody idiot," I all but shouted. Perhaps that wasn't the perfect thing to say under the circumstances, but she infuriated me.

I took a breath to calm down and saw everything in a flash.

"You have a way out, don't you?" I asked. I shook her by her wrist. "Don't you? You knew I'd follow you here." Gods, was her jealousy really so deep?

"Zinnia said—"

"Zinnia is dead. She was on *our* side in the end," I snapped. "Remember?"

Calla stuck her chin out, not an ounce of repentance.

"Do you really hate me that much?" I asked quietly.

"I don't hate you," she replied. "I just wanted to shine."

I shook my head. "I don't understand."

"You said it yourself, I have a way out." She looked uncertain, but with an edge of determination that creeped the shit out of me.

I frowned. "You let me get sucked in here, just so you could rescue me?" Saff was right, this was weirdest thing we'd done yet. "What if we don't get out?"

Her confidence wavered. "We have to…"

"Damn right we do," I snapped. "Although I'm not sure why I shouldn't leave you here." I sucked in a breath and blew it out hard through my nose. "Fine, how do you think we're getting out?"

She held up a trembling hand. In her fingers she held a golden sphere, with symbols etched on the surface.

I blinked. "What the hells?" I patted my pocket but found it empty. "You took the orb?" Was there no level of fucked up she wouldn't stoop to?

She smiled, a disturbing look. "It's all right, I can take you both with me. Or… maybe not."

I blinked. What the hells? Had she lost her mind?

"You didn't want to save me, did you?" I asked. "You just wanted to trap me in here. Why?"

"Why not?" she replied. "Now I have this, I can go wherever I like. I can do what I like. Maybe I'll go to the human realm and declare myself queen, as Myrta would have."

"You're insane," I told her.

"Maybe, but at least I won't be trapped in here for eternity." She eyed the orb and chose a symbol.

"I recommend the one to the seven hells," I said.

She laughed before she disappeared.

"Well shit," I said. "This is absolutely the last time I help her." As sisters went, she sucked pretty hard. As for me, I was done with being trusting and naive.

"Good idea," Saff said. "Now what?"

I looked him in the eyes and sagged. "To be honest, I have no idea. She took my plan to get out of here."

"Well, we'll need to find another way," he said firmly. "And if we can't, they will." He waved toward the guys and their worried faces.

"I hope so," I said wearily. "I really hope so. As much as I love you, I don't want to be here with you forever."

"Oh, I don't know. At least we wouldn't get interrupted." He cocked his head and gave me the sweetest smile I had ever seen on anyone.

"Yes, but there's no beer here," I pointed out.

"In that case—" He threw back his head and shouted. *"Get us out of here!"*

CHAPTER TWENTY-FOUR

I sat on what passed for ground here. It was strangely soft and smooth, but I felt as though it might drop out from under me at any moment.

"Should I try to blast our way out?" I asked.

"Begging the gods hasn't helped," Saff said. "And willing ourselves out didn't work."

I nodded. "Maybe we could shrink small enough to find a gap."

"That might be safer than a blast of magic," he said slowly. "I'd prefer not to be incinerated when it bounces."

"I'd prefer that to being here forever." I rose to my feet. "But let's use that as a last resort."

"Sounds like a plan." He took my hand. "I'd prefer a resort to this. Maybe one with a view of the ocean."

The sides of my mouth jerked upward. "Maybe we can go to one after this. We could lie back and relax with some of those drinks the humans like, with the paper umbrellas in them."

He grinned. "Yes! Fletcher was saying last night that his cousin Flynn lives in a place with lots of beaches, and drinks like that. Somewhere called —Hawaii?"

"Sounds perfect. Let's get out of here then." I began to shrink myself down as small as I could go. The frame of the mirror became bigger and bigger and the swirls of magic looked enormous enough to swallow us.

I kept hold of his hand and flew up to the top of the frame. "If we follow this along, we might find somewhere to slip through."

"Should we split up and look?" he asked. Even as the words came out of his mouth, he shook his head. "Better not. I don't want to lose you in here."

"I don't want to get lost," I agreed. "Let's go right first." I had no particular reason for the suggestion, but we had to start somewhere.

"Right," he replied. "Right it is."

We soared across the top of the frame and down the side.

"This thing looks airtight," he said, frustrated already.

"Be glad it's not," I told him, "or we'd run out of air."

"Good point. Across the bottom and the left side then."

We walked across the bottom slowly, then up the other side, but found no sign of a way out, not even a scratch in the ancient frame. Damn the amazing skill of the ancients. Apparently there were some scenarios even they hadn't foreseen.

"Blasting is starting to look like a viable option," he said as we landed and returned ourselves to our usual size.

My shoulders sagged. Despair started to rise inside my chest.

"What if that doesn't work?" I asked. "What if we really can get out of here?" Tears welled in my eyes. After everything we'd done, we'd succeeded in releasing nature magic, just to die? It didn't seem fair.

"Hey." Saff drew me into his arms and kissed the top of my head. "We will get out of here, I promise."

"How can you make a promise like that?" I rested

my head against his shoulder and let tears slide down my cheeks.

"Because I know us," he said firmly. "We always get through things. Remember when we first met and you got mad because Huon had talked about you so much? For a while there, I didn't think you would ever talk to me again. But you did. You saw how awesome I was and forgave me."

I gave a half laugh, half sob. "I remember. I was so pissed off with you both, I would have let Khat eat you when you fell down that hole and found him."

"I was so sad you were angry with me, I would have let him," Saff said with a laugh. "And we've been through a lot more since. Yina almost drowned me and then we got lost in the human realm. But here we are. And we won't stay here, we'll get out. We don't belong inside a magic mirror. If we have to shatter it to get out, we will."

"No, we don't." I sniffed. Something tickled the back of my mind. *If we have to shatter it...*

I straightened up. "You're right."

"I am?" He looked surprised, then pleased. "I am, of course I am. What am I right about?"

"Shattered things," I told him. I reached into my pocket and hoped like hells Calla hadn't somehow taken that as well. My fingertips brushed over the shard of glass. I pulled it out and held it up.

He blinked. "Isn't that…"

"Yes it is." I nodded.

He looked confused "No offence, but don't we need the rest of it?"

"Yes, but we have friends on the outside who could help with that." I gestured toward the guys, who hadn't moved from the front of the mirror.

"Oh. Well in that case, let's do it," he said brightly.

To be honest, I had no idea if this would work or not, but it was worth a try.

I held up the piece of glass in my fingers and waved to get the guy's attention.

They looked at each other, then back to me.

I pointed at the shard.

Huon said something, but I couldn't hear it. I pointed again, then mimed a round object with my other hand.

Kale mouthed, "Glass orb?" At least, I think that was what he said.

I nodded vigorously. "Yes, glass orb! Get the shards and bring them here!" For some reason I shouted, although I doubted they'd hear it any more than if I whispered.

Kale said something to Huon, who nodded. He waved Kale toward the doorway.

"Watch out for Calla!" I called out.

Huon looked at me in confusion and shook his head. He said something I couldn't make out.

I sighed. "It doesn't matter," I muttered. "Just be careful."

Saff put a hand on my shoulder. "They will," he said softly.

I leaned against him again. "I'm sorry for this. I shouldn't have tried to help her. I just—"

"She's your sister and you're nice," he said firmly. "I can't imagine you turning your back on her, or anyone. Even after your other sister took the throne and virtually enslaved the trolls, you still gave her the chance to redeem herself."

"And she did," I said softly. "I thought Calla had too."

Saff put his arms around me and rubbed my back lightly. "I know you did. It's not your fault she double-crossed you."

"It's my fault you're stuck in here because I wanted to believe she'd changed," I said.

"It's my fault I grabbed you at the last moment," he replied. "But I wouldn't change this for the realms. I have you all to myself and, try as they might, we can't hear them interrupt us." He kissed me soundly then, and deeply. His tongue ran over my lips and plunged into my mouth when I parted them for him.

"Do you think they'd mind watching?" he said between kisses.

I laughed softly. "I love you, but I'm not screwing inside a magic mirror. The gods only knows what doing that might do to us."

He clicked his tongue in disappointment, but leaned back and smiled. "Good point. We might create weird demon offspring in here."

"Right," I said. "Of all the demon offspring I might have, I wouldn't want weird ones."

He laughed. "I prefer weird to demon."

I thought about that for a moment. "Good point."

His head jerked up and he looked at something over my shoulder.

"What is it?" I turned to see Kale, a small bag in his hand.

"Did anyone order pieces of orb?" Saff asked and grinned.

"As a matter of fact, I did." I nodded. "I should have ordered some wine with it."

"Now we just have one more problem," Saff said. "How do we get that in here?"

"I suppose they'll have to will it in here." I cocked my head and watched the guys, apparently discussing exactly that.

Huon looked upset and shook his head at something Kale said. Fletcher gestured toward Kale, then at himself. Huon responded with something short and possibly angry. He pointed at Fletcher and made a cutting gesture across the air with his finger. Fletcher looked annoyed, but turned to Kale. The dark-skinned Fae looked like a mountain—unmovable. Whatever this was, he'd made up his mind.

Huon snapped something and stepped away.

"It looks like we'll get our answer," Saff said.

"And a visitor," I added. I preferred not to have anyone else stuck in here, but this might be the only way out.

Kale stood in front of the mirror, half closed his eyes and reached out.

The next thing I knew, he was beside me.

"Hey," Saff greeted. "Welcome to the inside of the mirror. Population, us."

Kale gave him a nod and handed me the bag. "This was all the cleanup Fae found. If it is not complete..."

"Then we're screwed," I finished for him. I sat on the floor, crossed my legs and opened the bag. I tipped the shards out and added the piece I had picked up on a whim.

"Myrta somehow used Calla's magic to bind this," I said slowly. "I suppose it's just the opposite of destroying things." I held my hand over the shards and focused on them all coming together to re-form a sphere. I thought it might take time, if it happened at all.

To my surprise, the pieces moved immediately. Within seconds, several were bound back together and other pieces swirled around as if they searched for the right place to go.

"Wow, that's impressive," Saff said. "And kinda hot."

"What can I say?" I asked, "I like balls."

Saff and Kale both chuckled.

"I would give that a nine," Kale remarked.

"Did you just make a joke?" Saff asked.

"Indeed," Kale replied.

"You don't think that was a ten?" I had to resist the urge to look up at them.

"It would be a ten, but there's only one," Kale replied.

"I had two, but one was stolen," I said dryly. "You didn't see my sister out there, did you? She has my other ball."

"I did not," Kale replied. "Nor did I see Tavar. I trust she can take care of herself."

"If anyone can, it's Tavar." I watched the last few pieces of glass circle the sphere several times. They appeared to be lost. Under other circumstances, I might have found it funny. Whoever heard of glass looking for its place in the world? Right now, though, I just wished they'd find it.

One piece sped up and skidded into a hole before it bound with the pieces around it. A moment later, another did the same.

"Last bit." It looked like the shard I had in my pocket. I held my breath. What if carrying it around had done something to it? I might have broken its connection to the rest of the orb forever. Then we would be—

Like a miniature glass bird, it flew to the last hole and all but threw itself inside.

"Good little shard," I told it.

It wriggled happily and then bound tightly with the glass around it.

"There, all done." I held the fully intact glass orb on my outstretched palm. "I'd feel better if this had symbols on it."

"It may not do what we're hoping it will," Saff pointed out.

"It could do bloody well anything," I admitted. "But Myrta needed it for something, so we can hope that something involved transporting around places."

Saff nodded. "Hand-holding time." He slipped him into my spare one and squeezed.

"If this works, I want a quiet spot and a lot of wine," I said. "All right, here goes."

I focused my thoughts and desires on the small sphere of glass and held my breath.

We shot out of the mirror so fast we narrowly missed knocking Fletcher on his ass. He stepped back at the last moment and we fell in a heap beside him.

"What do you know, it worked," Saff said.

Huon eyed me, brow creased in doubt. "Summer? Saff?"

I smiled and climbed to my feet. "It's me. Just me, no nasty Fae inhabiting my brain."

"Wouldn't a nasty Fae say that?" he asked.

I drew my lips over to one side of my mouth. "The first time we screwed was after a huge fight. You called me a brat. I called you an asshole."

He grinned slowly. "We were both right."

I snorted a laugh. "You're not so bad." I gave him

an embrace and a kiss on his mouth, then did the same to Fletcher, who wore a shocked look on his face.

"You got out of there," he stated.

"Yes," I replied. "Yes we did. Thanks to Kale for getting the rest of the orb." I opened my hand and blinked. "Um…"

The orb now glowed with yellow-brown light and swirls of black. I looked from it to the mirror. In its glassy surface, I saw my face. My hair was a mess and my eyes a little wild, but it was still me. I touched my cheek with my fingertips. My reflection did the same.

"It's just a mirror," I said, confused.

Kale peered into it. "It would appear so," he agreed. "Your ball seems to absorb dark magic."

"And then what?" I asked rhetorically. "Is this going to explode and kill us all after all?"

Kale rubbed the top of his head and looked at the orb for a long moment or two. "I think not. It seems stable enough. Perhaps see if it will absorb magic from something else."

"The sword," Saff said immediately. "Please try the sword. Then I can keep it afterward."

"If you think I'm letting you keep an object which has been infused with dark magic—" Huon started.

"I have a problem with the idea of Saff having anything pointy," Fletcher said. "Apart from the one in his pants."

Saff pouted playfully. "What if I promise not to poke it into anyone?"

"The sword or your cock?" I asked.

"The sword," Saff said. "I'll happily poke my cock into any one of you." He batted his eyelashes at Fletcher, who flushed.

"No sword," Huon said firmly. "But let's see if the magic can be removed from it."

"Easy for you to say," I muttered. Still, I approached the sword and touched the orb to it. I flinched when magic flared on the blade, but it slithered into the orb and left the steel to shine.

"Still no explosion," I said. "If this can hold all the dark magic, we won't have to worry about anyone using these objects again." We would just have to worry about the orb itself.

"Try the book," Huon suggested.

"Take care," Kale warned. "Tomes hold great power of their own. This one has so much I can almost feel it."

I nodded. "So can I." The book made my skin crawl in a way no other book ever had. I swallowed and stepped over to it.

Before I could even touch the pages, they opened and began to flick over. Page after page, after page. When each turned, dark magic roiled off the paper. Words I couldn't read slid away and left the pages blank. When it finally fell still, the orb felt heavier, but steady.

"I feel a little bad for erasing all of that," I remarked. "I bet that took the author years to write."

"Perhaps they should have written novels instead of dark magic spells then," Huon said dryly.

"True." I stepped over to the circlet and sucked away its magic, then that of the handful of other objects in the room.

By the time I was done, the room felt lighter, but the stone on the walls seemed older, more worn.

"I think we need to get out of here," I said. "I have a feeling only the dark magic was holding this place together." A rumble punctuated my words.

"But the sword—" Saff said.

"Leave it and get your ass up those stairs," Huon growled. "Before I kick it all the way up."

"Fine," Saff grumbled, but trotted toward the door.

I followed, with Kale and Fletcher close behind. I held the orb close to my chest. Gods forbid I would fall and break it. The last thing we needed was to have dark magic loose in the Fae realm. We would be more doomed than we were before.

The ground moved under my feet and I had to grab hold of Kale's arm to stay upright. Pieces of rock started to fall from the ceiling.

Frantic, I shouted, "We need to shrink to get through the—"

Ahead of us, a section of wall crumbled and fell outward, exposing us to bright daylight.

"Crack," I finished.

"Fly!" Huon ordered.

I didn't need to be told twice. I threw out my wings and leapt as the tunnel collapsed on itself.

Fletcher gave a startled cry. Huon had grabbed him and taken off just before the walls crashed down around them. Thank the gods Huon had the where-withal to save Fletcher as well as himself.

With a crash that shook the land around us for kilometres, the rest of the tunnels gave way and sank in on themselves.

My heart raced. The orb in my hand pulsed. "There's no going back into those artefacts now," I told the magic.

"Dear gods!" Huon called out.

"What?" I did a slow turn in the air and looked in the same direction he gazed.

"Well, well," Saff said.

"What the hells?" I lowered myself slowly, a good distance from the ruins and stared around me.

Where before, the trapdoor had stood in a desolate field, it now stood amongst small, but strongly growing grass. Saplings dotted the area. Some already bore buds.

Tears slid down my cheeks.

"We did it," I said softly.

Huon moved to stand beside me and took my hand. "Yes, we did."

"Birch would be proud of you," I told him.

"You too," he said. "You know, he always wanted us to get together."

"I told him we never would." I laughed. "I guess he knew more than I did."

"He was wiser than all of us," he agreed.

"You'll be that wise," I assured him. "Some day, and if you listen to me a lot."

He threw back his head and laughed.

"This is quite something," Kale said. He stepped to the other side of me and I slipped my hand into his.

"We couldn't have done it without you," I told him. "And Saff and Fletcher." I smiled at both guys.

"There you are." Rick came out from behind a

stand of trees which were covered in unfurling leaves. "We found someone you might know."

Tavar stepped out behind him, one arm around Calla, her blade to my sister's throat.

Tiny trotted beside Jude, who was inexplicably dirty.

"Tavar chased Calla. Tiny and I tackled her," Jude explained.

"It seems my blade also stops Fae from shrinking," Tavar remarked easily.

Calla swallowed visibly. "I'm sorry, I wasn't going to—"

I rolled my eyes. "Yes, you were. Where is the gold orb?"

She eyed the one in my hand and her face paled. "You have the..."

"Yes, I do, don't I?" I was tempted to toss the orb in the air, just to see the look on her face, but thought better of it.

"That's dangerous," she said.

"What, this?" I shrugged. "It's just a bit of glass."

"No, what's inside." Her voice was high, bordering on panic. "Dark magic. The gods themselves..."

I frowned. "What about the gods themselves?"

Calla gaped, but didn't respond. She averted her

eyes. I wanted to slap her and force her to tell me what she knew.

In the end, it wasn't necessary.

"Legend has it, dark magic was stolen from the gods," Tavar said easily.

"Oh really?" I raised my eyebrows. "In that case..."

"No!" Calla must have guessed my intentions when I took a step toward her.

"It doesn't belong to us," I said. "It doesn't belong here. There's no Fae or human in any realm I trust with dark magic. Especially you."

She flinched. A fat tear rolled down her cheek. "I swear, I never—"

"Save it." I pulled the golden orb from her fingers and stepped away. I smiled at Kale. "Do I get a ten now? I have a ball in either hand."

He inclined his head. "You hold more power in your hands than any living Fae has ever done. I would give you whatever number you asked for."

I frowned. "That wasn't quite what I meant."

"You're my ten," Fletcher said. "Whoever's balls you're holding at the time."

"Same here," Saff said. "Preferably mine though."

"I tend to agree with them," Huon said. "We all make a great team. Now, can you get rid of those balls? You're making me nervous."

I laughed softly. "Fine. Stand back then."

I worked my finger up the side of the golden orb and pressed the symbol for the seven hells. As before, the sky opened up above us, swirling clouds, darkness and hot wind.

"Hey, gods, take you shitty dark magic back!" I shouted. I drew back my arm and threw the glass orb as hard as I could into the clouds.

"No!" Calla wrenched herself away from Tavar and lunged toward the gate.

"Cal—" I called. I reached for her arm as she flew past, but she disappeared into the clouds, along with the orb.

"Well, shit," I muttered. I should have seen that coming too, I supposed. To be honest, I had no idea how she would have been dealt with anyway. Locking up Fae was notoriously difficult. Still, she was my sister, if only by blood.

I swallowed. I would mourn her later. In the meantime, I had one last thing to do.

"I guess we don't need this now either." I swapped the golden orb into my other hand and threw it after the first one. It too was sucked away and the gate closed, leaving blue sky and sunshine.

I wiped my hands on each other. "I suppose that's that then."

"There is a little matter of getting Jude and I home," Rick said and scowled as if all of this was my fault.

I smiled back at him. "The veil should be open again now. Taking you home should be easy."

"If it's okay, I might stay awhile," Jude said. "There's nothing back home for me, and Tiny seems to like it here."

Huon nodded. "Of course, you're welcome to stay."

"I'm going through the veil to find my mate," Khat declared. He slunk out from behind the trees. Were they still growing? The realm would be green again in no time at this rate.

"Good luck," I told him. "And thanks for your help."

"Finally, some gratitude," he replied.

"I'm going to find my people," Tavar said. "We have forests to reclaim and the silver Fae have invited us to see their kingdom.

I nodded and stepped over to give her a hug. "Come back any time. I'm going to miss you."

She surprised me by giving me a smile and returning my hug. "You're welcome in troll territory any time."

"You won't be eating any more mimicats, will you?" I asked, half-joking.

She snorted. "I think perhaps we will find other things to eat. Screamspinners maybe."

I wrinkled my nose. "Better you than me."

She stepped back, gave me a nod and disappeared into the trees.

I watched the leaves fall back into place behind her and smiled.

"All right my loves, let's go and get roaring drunk." I hooked my arms around Huon and Fletcher's and sighed.

"Let's do it," Saff said happily.

"Yes, that too." I laughed.

Legend has it, human girls dream about their wedding day. The same could be said for Fae girls, but we get married much older. I'd just turned one hundred and twenty-four years old, even though I looked like a human of about twenty-four.

I didn't wear white, like humans do, but green, with a garland of flowers on my hair. My feet were bare, but my heart was full.

Most folk spend years and years hoping to find the right mate to spend the rest of their lives with, and I found four.

Huon, with white flowers on his blonde hair, smiled as the harp began to play. Saff, with a riot of colourful flowers on his red hair, rolled from his heels to the balls of his feet. Beside him, Fletcher wore no flowers, but had a piece of fabric around his neck. A tie, he'd called it.

Kale stood on the other side of Fletcher, also with no flowers on his head, but vines instead. He nodded at me and I smiled back.

I walked slowly toward them. I wanted to savour this moment for as long as I could. Maybe I should have done this a guy at a time, but we'd agreed this was better. For a crazy week or so, last year, we'd been through the wildest ride a Fae could ever imagine, and we had done it together.

We would do this together too.

"Please approach," the celebrant said. She held out a white ribbon to me. I held out my wrists and let her wind it once around them.

"King Huon." She nodded to him.

He strode forward. Every bit the confident king. He had his throne back, and the adoration of all the Fae. He might even be as loved as Birch was, in his day. He was certainly treated like a hero. We all were. Some days it got so much we had to sneak off and hide in the river, under the bower of roses, their petals now as strong and pure as their scent.

Huon grinned at me as the ribbon was wound once around his wrists as well.

"Saff."

With a huge grin, Saff walked forward and allowed his wrists to be added to the chain. Tears shone in his eyes too. He, of all of us, was the only one who didn't mind all the attention. He'd become a favourite with the children, who pestered him with questions all day. He answered every single one of them.

"Kale."

Kale started writing his book about our journey. He wouldn't let anyone read his draft, but promised we'd all get a copy when it was done. We joked people would think it was fiction. Who would believe such a wild story if they hadn't lived it?

"Fletcher."

Fletcher went back to the human realm long enough to officially quit his job, and see his brother settled. Somehow, the boat turned up at the aquarium, and no one seemed to suspect a thing. So, Rick kept his job, but I suspected he'd spend his time looking out for another Seafae. And being a grumpy ass. That would never change. At least he kept us stocked with coffee and Nutella whenever we dropped by to visit. He always had both on hand. I suspected he did it to make sure we would keep dropping in. We always would. He was one of us, after all.

Each of my guys in turn had the long ribbon wound around their wrists, until it bound us all to each other.

Forever.

"You are joined," the celebrant said. "One and all, all and one, until the day you go to the arms of the gods."

The crowd let out a cheer.

Tears trickled down my cheeks. Happy tears.

I cried a lot these days.

I'm told pregnancy will do that to a woman.

The end

Maggie Alabaster is a reverse harem and fantasy romance author.

She lives in NSW, Australia with one spouse, two daughters, dog, cat, rabbits and countless birds.

Sign up for my newsletter! Sign Up!

Join my reader group! Join here!

Follow me on Bookbub! Click here to follow me!

Court of Blood and Binding

Book 1 Song of Scent and Magic

Book 2 Crown of Mist and Heat

Book 3 Sword of Balm and Shadow

Book 4 Whisper of Frost and Flame

Dark Masque

Book 1 Bait

Book 2 Prey

Book 3 Trap

Saving Abbie

Book 1 Pitch

Book 2 Pound

Book 3 Session

Book 4 Muse

Book 5 Rhythm

Book 6 Encore

Novella Venomous

Ruthless Claws

Book 1 Ivory

Book 2 Crimson

Book 3 Elodie

Harmony's Magic

Book 1 Summoned by Fire

Book 2 Summoned by Fate

Book 3 Summoned by Desire

Shifter's Vault

Book 1 Discarded

Book 2 Deceived

Book 3 Disgraced

My Alien Mates

Book 1 Star Warriors

Book 2 Star Defenders

Book 3 Star Protectors

Academy of Modern Magic

Book 1 Digital Magic

Book 2 Virtual Magic

Book 3 Logical Magic

Complete Collection

Summer's Harem

Book 1: Shimmer

Book 2: Glimmer

Book 3: Flicker

Complete collection

Short reads

Taken by the Snowmen

Jingle All the Way

Also by Maggie Alabaster and Erin Yoshikawa

Caught by the Tide

Book 1–Pursued by Shadows

Book 2 Pursued by Darkness

Book 3 Pursued by Monsters